DOVER · THRIFT · EDITIONS

Selected
Canterbury Tales

GEOFFREY CHAUCER

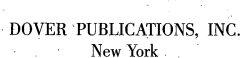

DOVER PUBLICATIONS, INC.
New York

DOVER THRIFT EDITIONS

GENERAL EDITOR: STANLEY APPELBAUM
EDITOR OF THIS VOLUME: CANDACE WARD

Copyright

Bibliographical Note

This Dover edition, first published in 1994, is a new selection of unabridged tales as they originally appeared in *Canterbury Tales: Rendered into Modern English by J. U. Nicolson*, published by Garden City Publishing Company, Inc., New York, in 1934. A new introductory Note and footnotes have been specially prepared for this edition.

Library of Congress Cataloging-in-Publication Data

Chaucer, Geoffrey, d. 1400.
   [Canterbury tales. Selections]
   Selected Canterbury tales / Geoffrey Chaucer.
       p.   cm. — (Dover thrift editions)
   ISBN-13: 978-0-486-28241-1
   ISBN-10: 0-486-28241-4
   1. Christian pilgrims and pilgrimages—England—Canterbury—Poetry.
2. Tales, Medieval.   I. Title.   II. Series.
PR1867   1994
821'.1—dc20
                                                                94–35008
                                                                    CIP

Manufactured in the United States by Courier Corporation
28241414
www.doverpublications.com

Note

During his lifetime — at least according to the historical records — Geoffrey Chaucer (1343?–1400) was better known for his civil service than for his literary output. He began his career as a page in the aristocratic household of Lionel of Antwerp, a son of King Edward III; in 1359, while serving as a soldier at the Siege of Reims, he was captured by the French and later ransomed by the King. He traveled to Spain, Italy, France and Flanders in a variety of diplomatic capacities, and over the years, he filled a number of government posts, including Controller of the Customs and Subsidies on Wool, Justice of the Peace and Knight of the Shire (member of Parliament) for the county of Kent, Clerk of the King's Works, and deputy forester of the King's park in North Petherton, Somerset. Despite his connections with the aristocracy, Chaucer remained closely tied to the large and increasingly important middle class into which he was born. The two perspectives — that of a well-educated, well-connected courtier and that of a pragmatic businessman — inform Chaucer's writings, providing a balance between the romance and philosophy of the upper classes and the workaday reality of London commerce.

Of Chaucer's works, including the *Book of the Duchess* (1369–1370), *Parlement of Foules* (c. 1382), *Troilus and Criseyde* (c. 1385), and *The Canterbury Tales*, the latter is probably the most famous. Begun in 1386, Chaucer sets his tales within a frame narrative. A group of pilgrims meet at the Tabard Inn in Southwark, and decide to travel together to the shrine of Thomas à Becket. The host of the inn, Harry Bailly, suggests that each of the pilgrims "shal telle tales tweye [two]/ To Canterbury-ward . . ./ And homward he shal tellen othere two,/ Of adventures that whilom han bifalle [once upon a time have befallen]." Whoever recited the best tale would be treated to a grand supper by the others when they returned to the Tabard Inn.

Though the use of a narrative frame was not original to *The Canterbury Tales*, Chaucer's poem was unique in its application of the device. By having each pilgrim tell his own tale, Chaucer was able to use the stories to reflect the personality of the teller. In addition, the tales are punctuated by exchanges between the pilgrims, which adds yet another dimension to the work. Thus, Chaucer complicates the framing device by interweaving the frame fiction with the stories told by the pilgrims — each enhancing the other, adding depth and drama to the poem. The result is a brilliant portrait of both types and highly individualized characters who bring Chaucer's world of fourteenth-century England to life.

Though Chaucer worked on *The Canterbury Tales* the last fourteen years of his life, he completed only twenty-two of the intended one hundred twenty tales.

Contents

FROM THE GENERAL PROLOGUE[1]

HERE BYGYNNETH THE BOOK OF THE TALES OF CAUNTERBURY

WHAN that Aprille with his shoures soote
The droghte of March hath perced to the roote,
And bathed every veyne in swich licour,
Of which vertu engendred is the flour;
Whan Zephirus eek with his sweete breeth
Inspired hath in every holt and heeth
The tendre croppes, and the yonge sonne
Hath in the Ram his halfe cours yronne,
And smale foweles maken melodye,
That slepen al the nyght with open eye,
So priketh hem nature in hir corages;
Thanne longen folk to goon on pilgrimages,
And palmeres for to seken straunge strondes,
To ferne halwes, kowthe in sondry londes;
And specially, from every shires ende
Of Engelond, to Caunterbury they wende,
The hooly blisful martir for to seke,
That hem hath holpen whan that they were seeke.
    Bifil that in that seson on a day,
In Southwerk at the Tabard as I lay,
Redy to wenden on my pilgrymage
To Caunterbury with ful devout corage,
At nyght were come into that hostelrye
Wel nyne and twenty in a compaignye,
Of sondry folk, by aventure yfalle
In felaweshipe, and pilgrimes were they alle,
That toward Caunterbury wolden ryde.

1. An example of Chaucer's Middle English verse.

The chambres and the stables weren wyde,
And wel we weren esed atte beste.
And shortly, whan the sonne was to reste,
So hadde I spoken with hem everichon
That I was of hir felaweshipe anon,
And made forward erly for to ryse,
To take oure wey ther as I yow devyse.

THE GENERAL PROLOGUE

HERE BEGINS THE BOOK OF THE
TALES OF CANTERBURY

WHEN APRIL with his showers sweet with fruit
    The drought of March has pierced unto the root
And bathed each vein with liquor that has power
To generate therein and sire the flower;
When Zephyr also has, with his sweet breath,
Quickened again, in every holt and heath,
The tender shoots and buds, and the young sun
Into the Ram one half his course has run,
And many little birds make melody
That sleep through all the night with open eye
(So Nature pricks them on to ramp and rage) —
Then do folk long to go on pilgrimage,
And palmers to go seeking out strange strands,
To distant shrines well known in sundry lands.
And specially from every shire's end
Of England they to Canterbury wend,
The holy blessed martyr[1] there to seek
Who helped them when they lay so ill and weak.
   Befell that, in that season, on a day
In Southwark, at the Tabard, as I lay
Ready to start upon my pilgrimage
To Canterbury, full of devout homage,
There came at nightfall to that hostelry
Some nine and twenty in a company
Of sundry persons who had chanced to fall
In fellowship, and pilgrims were they all
That toward Canterbury town would ride.
The rooms and stables spacious were and wide,
And well we there were eased, and of the best.

---

1. *holy blessed martyr*] St. Thomas à Becket, Archbishop of Canterbury, who was murdered by four knights of Henry II's court in 1170.

And briefly, when the sun had gone to rest,
So had I spoken with them, every one,
That I was of their fellowship anon,
And made agreement that we'd early rise
To take the road, as you I will apprise.
    But none the less, whilst I have time and space,
Before yet farther in this tale I pace,
It seems to me accordant with reason
To inform you of the state of every one
Of all of these, as it appeared to me,
And who they were, and what was their degree,
And even how arrayed there at the inn;
And with a knight thus will I first begin.

The Knight

A knight there was, and he a worthy man,
Who, from the moment that he first began
To ride about the world, loved chivalry,
Truth, honour, freedom and all courtesy.
Full worthy was he in his liege-lord's war,
And therein had he ridden (none more far)
As well in Christendom as heathenesse,
And honoured everywhere for worthiness.
    At Alexandria, he, when it was won;
Full oft the table's roster he'd begun
Above all nations' knights in Prussia.
In Latvia raided he, and Russia,
No christened man so oft of his degree.
In far Granada at the siege was he
Of Algeciras, and in Belmarie.[2]
At Ayas was he and at Satalye[3]
When they were won; and on the Middle Sea
At many a noble meeting chanced to be.
Of mortal battles he had fought fifteen,
And he'd fought for our faith at Tramissene[4]

2. *Belmarie*] Benimarim (the name of a tribe), in Morocco.
3. *Satalye*] modern Adalia, in Asia Minor.
4. *Tramissene*] modern Tlemçen, in Algeria.

Three times in lists, and each time slain his foe.
This self-same worthy knight had been also
At one time with the lord of Palatye[5]
Against another heathen in Turkey:
And always won he sovereign fame for prize.
Though so illustrious, he was very wise
And bore himself as meekly as a maid.
He never yet had any vileness said,
In all his life, to whatsoever wight.
He was a truly perfect, gentle knight.
But now, to tell you all of his array,
His steeds were good, but yet he was not gay.
Of simple fustian wore he a jupon[6]
Sadly discoloured by his habergeon;[7]
For he had lately come from his voyage
And now was going on this pilgrimage.

The Squire

With him there was his son, a youthful squire,
A lover and a lusty bachelor,
With locks well curled, as if they'd laid in press.
Some twenty years of age he was, I guess.
In stature he was of an average length,
Wondrously active, aye, and great of strength.
He'd ridden sometime with the cavalry
In Flanders, in Artois, and Picardy,
And borne him well within that little space
In hope to win thereby his lady's grace.
Prinked[8] out he was, as if he were a mead,
All full of fresh-cut flowers white and red.
Singing he was, or fluting, all the day;
He was as fresh as is the month of May.
Short was his gown, with sleeves both long and wide.
Well could he sit on horse, and fairly ride.

5. *Palatye*] modern Balat.
6. *jupon*] jacket or tunic.
7. *habergeon*] a jacket of mail.
8. *Prinked*] primped; adorned.

He could make songs and words thereto indite,
Joust, and dance too, as well as sketch and write.
So hot he loved that, while night told her tale,
He slept no more than does a nightingale.
Courteous he, and humble, willing and able,
And carved before his father at the table.

The Yeoman

A yeoman had he,[9] nor more servants, no,
At that time, for he chose to travel so;
And he was clad in coat and hood of green.
A sheaf of peacock arrows bright and keen
Under his belt he bore right carefully
(Well could he keep his tackle yeomanly:
His arrows had no draggled feathers low),
And in his hand he bore a mighty bow.
A cropped head had he and a sun-browned face.
Of woodcraft knew he all the useful ways.
Upon his arm he bore a bracer gay,
And at one side a sword and buckler, yea,
And at the other side a dagger bright,
Well sheathed and sharp as spear point in the light;
On breast a Christopher[10] of silver sheen.
He bore a horn in baldric[11] all of green;
A forester he truly was, I guess.

The Prioress

There was also a nun, a prioress,
Who, in her smiling, modest was and coy;
Her greatest oath was but "By Saint Eloy!"
And she was known as Madam Eglantine.
Full well she sang the services divine,
Intoning through her nose, becomingly;
And fair she spoke her French, and fluently,

9. *he*] that is, the Knight.
10. *Christopher*] an image of Saint Christopher.
11. *baldric*] a belt worn over one shoulder to support a sword or horn.

After the school of Stratford-at-the-Bow,
For French of Paris was not hers to know.
At table she had been well taught withal,
And never from her lips let morsels fall,
Nor dipped her fingers deep in sauce, but ate
With so much care the food upon her plate
That never driblet fell upon her breast.
In courtesy she had delight and zest.
Her upper lip was always wiped so clean
That in her cup was no iota seen
Of grease, when she had drunk her draught of wine.
Becomingly she reached for meat to dine.
And certainly delighting in good sport,
She was right pleasant, amiable — in short.
She was at pains to counterfeit the look
Of courtliness, and stately manners took,
And would be held worthy of reverence.
  But, to say something of her moral sense,
She was so charitable and piteous
That she would weep if she but saw a mouse
Caught in a trap, though it were dead or bled.
She had some little dogs, too, that she fed
On roasted flesh, or milk and fine white bread.
But sore she'd weep if one of them were dead,
Or if men smote it with a rod to smart:
For pity ruled her, and her tender heart.
Right decorous her pleated wimple was;
Her nose was fine; her eyes were blue as glass;
Her mouth was small and therewith soft and red;
But certainly she had a fair forehead;
It was almost a full span broad, I own,
For, truth to tell, she was not undergrown.
Neat was her cloak, as I was well aware.
Of coral small about her arm she'd bear
A string of beads and gauded[12] all with green;
And therefrom hung a brooch of golden sheen
Whereon there was first written a crowned "A,"
And under, *Amor vincit omnia.*[13]

---

12. *gauded*] in a rosary the beads marking divisions are called gauds.
13. Amor vincit omnia] Love conquers all.

The Nun

Another little nun with her had she,

The Three Priests

Who was her chaplain; and of priests she'd three.

The Monk

A monk there was, one made for mastery,
An outrider,[14] who loved his venery;
A manly man, to be an abbot able.
Full many a blooded horse had he in stable:
And when he rode men might his bridle hear
A-jingling in the whistling wind as clear,
Aye, and as loud as does the chapel bell
Where this brave monk was master of the cell.
The rule of Maurus or Saint Benedict,
By reason it was old and somewhat strict,
This said monk let such old things slowly pace
And followed new-world manners in their place.
He cared not for that text a clean-plucked hen
Which holds that hunters are not holy men;
Nor that a monk, when he is cloisterless,
Is like unto a fish that's waterless;
That is to say, a monk out of his cloister.
But this same text he held not worth an oyster;
And I said his opinion was right good.
What? Should he study as a madman would
Upon a book in cloister cell? Or yet
Go labour with his hands and swink[15] and sweat,
As Austin[16] bids? How shall the world be served?
Let Austin have his toil to him reserved.
Therefore he was a rider day and night;

14. *outrider*] a monk privileged to ride abroad on the business of his order.
15. *swink*] toil, slave.
16. *Austin*] Saint Augustine.

Greyhounds he had, as swift as bird in flight.
Since riding and the hunting of the hare
Were all his love, for no cost would he spare.
I saw his sleeves were purfled[17] at the hand
With fur of grey, the finest in the land;
Also, to fasten hood beneath his chin,
He had of good wrought gold a curious pin:
A love-knot in the larger end there was.
His head was bald and shone like any glass,
And smooth as one anointed was his face.
Fat was this lord, he stood in goodly case.
His bulging eyes he rolled about, and hot
They gleamed and red, like fire beneath a pot;
His boots were soft; his horse of great estate.
Now certainly he was a fine prelate:
He was not pale as some poor wasted ghost.
A fat swan loved he best of any roast.
His palfrey[18] was as brown as is a berry.

The Friar

A friar there was, a wanton and a merry,
A limiter,[19] a very festive man.
In all the Orders Four is none that can
Equal his gossip and his fair language.
He had arranged full many a marriage
Of women young, and this at his own cost.
Unto his order he was a noble post.[20]
Well liked by all and intimate was he
With franklins everywhere in his country,
And with the worthy women of the town:
For at confessing he'd more power in gown
(As he himself said) than a good curate,
For of his order he was licentiate.
He heard confession gently, it was said,

17. *purfled*] trimmed, decorated.
18. *palfrey*] a saddle horse other than a war-horse.
19. *limiter*] a friar licensed to beg within a certain district — within limits.
20. *post*] a pillar.

Gently absolved too, leaving naught of dread.
He was an easy man to give penance
When knowing he should gain a good pittance;
For to a begging friar, money given
Is sign that any man has been well shriven.
For if one gave (he dared to boast of this),
He took the man's repentance not amiss.
For many a man there is so hard of heart
He cannot weep however pains may smart.
Therefore, instead of weeping and of prayer,
Men should give silver to poor friars all bare.
His tippet[21] was stuck always full of knives
And pins, to give to young and pleasing wives.
And certainly he kept a merry note:
Well could he sing and play upon the rote.
At balladry he bore the prize away.
His throat was white as lily of the May;
Yet strong he was as ever champion.
In towns he knew the taverns, every one,
And every good host and each barmaid too —
Better than begging lepers, these he knew.
For unto no such solid man as he
Accorded it, as far as he could see,
To have sick lepers for acquaintances.
There is no honest advantageousness
In dealing with such poverty-stricken curs;
It's with the rich and with big victuallers.
And so, wherever profit might arise,
Courteous he was and humble in men's eyes.
There was no other man so virtuous.
He was the finest beggar of his house;
A certain district being farmed to him,
None of his brethren dared approach its rim;
For though a widow had no shoes to show,
So pleasant was his *In principio*,[22]
He always got a farthing ere he went.
He lived by pickings, it is evident.
And he could romp as well as any whelp.

21. *tippet*] scarf.
22. In principio] "In the beginning," the opening of the Gospel of St. John, which was
credited with almost magical powers.

On love days[23] could he be of mickle[24] help.
For there he was not like a cloisterer,
With threadbare cope[25] as is the poor scholar,
But he was like a lord or like a pope.
Of double worsted was his semi-cope,
That rounded like a bell, as you may guess.
He lisped a little, out of wantonness,
To make his English soft upon his tongue;
And in his harping, after he had sung,
His two eyes twinkled in his head as bright
As do the stars within the frosty night.
This worthy limiter was named Hubert.

The Merchant

There was a merchant with forked beard, and girt
In motley gown, and high on horse he sat,
Upon his head a Flemish beaver hat;
His boots were fastened rather elegantly.
His spoke his notions out right pompously,
Stressing the times when he had won, not lost.
He would the sea were held at any cost
Across from Middleburgh to Orwell town.
At money-changing he could make a crown.
This worthy man kept all his wits well set;
There was no one could say he was in debt,
So well he governed all his trade affairs
With bargains and with borrowings and with shares.
Indeed, he was a worthy man withal,
But, sooth to say, his name I can't recall.

The Clerk

A clerk from Oxford was with us also,
Who'd turned to getting knowledge, long ago.

23. *love days*] days appointed for the settling of disputes by arbitration.
24. *mickle*] great, much.
25. *cope*] a long, enveloping ecclesiastical garment.

As meagre was his horse as is a rake,
Nor he himself too fat, I'll undertake,
But he looked hollow and went soberly.
Right threadbare was his overcoat; for he
Had got him yet no churchly benefice,
Nor was so worldly as to gain office.
For he would rather have at his bed's head
Some twenty books, all bound in black and red,
Of Aristotle and his philosophy
Than rich robes, fiddle, or gay psaltery.
Yet, and for all he was philosopher,
He had but little gold within his coffer;
But all that he might borrow from a friend
On books and learning he would swiftly spend,
And then he'd pray right busily for the souls
Of those who gave him wherewithal for schools.
Of study took he utmost care and heed.
Not one word spoke he more than was his need;
And that was said in fullest reverence,
And short and quick and full of high good sense.
Pregnant of moral virtue was his speech;
And gladly would he learn and gladly teach.

The Lawyer

A sergeant[26] of the law, wary and wise,
Who'd often gone to Paul's walk to advise,
There was also, compact of excellence.
Discreet he was, and of great reverence;
At least he seemed so, his words were so wise.
Often he sat as justice in assize,
By patent or commission from the crown;
Because of learning and his high renown,
He took large fees and many robes could own.
So great a purchaser[27] was never known.

26. *sergeant*] in English law, a barrister of the highest rank.
27. *purchaser*] one who acquires lands by means other than descent or inheritance.

All was fee simple to him, in effect,
Wherefore his claims could never be suspect.
Nowhere a man so busy of his class,
And yet he seemed much busier than he was.
All cases and all judgments could he cite
That from King William's time were apposite.
And he could draw a contract so explicit
Not any man could fault therefrom elicit;
And every statute he'd verbatim quote.
He rode but badly in a medley coat,
Belted in a silken sash, with little bars,
But of his dress no more particulars.

The Franklin

There was a franklin in his company;
White was his beard as is the white daisy.
Of sanguine temperament by every sign,
He loved right well his morning sop in wine.
Delightful living was the goal he'd won,
For he was Epicurus' very son,
That held opinion that a full delight
Was true felicity, perfect and right.
A householder, and that a great, was he;
Saint Julian[28] he was in his own country.
His bread and ale were always right well done;
A man with better cellars there was none.
Baked meat was never wanting in his house,
Of fish and flesh, and that so plenteous
It seemed to snow therein both food and drink
Of every dainty that a man could think.
According to the season of the year
He changed his diet and his means of cheer.
Full many a fattened partridge did he mew,

28. *Saint Julian*] the patron saint of hospitality.

And many a bream and pike in fish-pond too.
Woe to his cook, except the sauces were
Poignant and sharp, and ready all his gear.
His table, waiting in his hall alway,
Stood ready covered through the livelong day.
At county sessions was he lord and sire,
And often acted as a knight of shire.
A dagger and a trinket-bag of silk
Hung from his girdle, white as morning milk.
He had been sheriff and been auditor;
And nowhere was a worthier vavasor.[29]

The Haberdasher and the Carpenter

A haberdasher and a carpenter,

The Weaver, the Dyer, and the Arras-Maker

An arras-maker, dyer, and weaver
Were with us, clothed in similar livery,
All of one sober, great fraternity.
Their gear was new and well adorned it was;
Their weapons were not cheaply trimmed with brass,
But all with silver; chastely made and well
Their girdles and their pouches too, I tell.
Each man of them appeared a proper burgess
To sit in guildhall on a high dais.
And each of them, for wisdom he could span,
Was fitted to have been an alderman;
For chattels they'd enough, and, too, of rent;
To which their goodwives gave a free assent,
Or else for certain they had been to blame.
It's good to hear "Madam" before one's name,
And go to church when all the world may see,
Having one's mantle borne right royally.

---

29. *vavasor*] a sub-vassal, next in rank below a baron.

The Cook

A cook they had with them, just for the nonce,
To boil the chickens with the marrow-bones,
And flavour tartly and with galingale.[30]
Well could he tell a draught of London ale.
And he could roast and seethe and broil and fry,
And make a good thick soup, and bake a pie.
But very ill it was, it seemed to me,
That on his shin a deadly sore had he;
For sweet blanc-mange,[31] he made it with the best.

The Sailor

There was a sailor, living far out west;
For aught I know, he was of Dartmouth town.
He sadly rode a hackney, in a gown,
Of thick rough cloth falling to the knee.
A dagger hanging on a cord had he
About his neck, and under arm, and down.
The summer's heat had burned his visage brown;
And certainly he was a good fellow.
Full many a draught of wine he'd drawn, I trow,
Of Bordeaux vintage, while the trader[32] slept.
Nice conscience was a thing he never kept.
If that he fought and got the upper hand,
By water he sent them home to every land.
But as for craft, to reckon well his tides,
His currents and the dangerous watersides,
His harbours, and his moon, his pilotage,
There was none such from Hull to far Carthage.
Hardy, and wise in all things undertaken,
By many a tempest had his beard been shaken.

30. *galingale*] a kind of sedge with an aromatic root.
31. *blanc-mange*] not akin to the modern dish, but a compound of minced capon, with
    cream, sugar and flour.
32. *trader*] that is, his passenger.

He knew well all the havens, as they were,
From Gottland to the Cape of Finisterre,
And every creek in Brittany and Spain;
His vessel had been christened *Madeleine*.

The Physician

With us there was a doctor of physic;
In all this world was none like him to pick
For talk of medicine and surgery;
For he was grounded in astronomy.[33]
He often kept a patient from the pall
By horoscopes and magic natural.
Well could he tell the fortune ascendent
Within the houses for his sick patient.
He knew the cause of every malady,
Were it of hot or cold, of moist or dry,
And where engendered, and of what humour;
He was a very good practitioner.
The cause being known, down to the deepest root,
Anon he gave to the sick man his boot.[34]
Ready he was, with his apothecaries,
To send him drugs and all electuaries;
By mutual aid much gold they'd always won —
Their friendship was a thing not new begun.
Well read was he in Esculapius,
And Deiscorides, and in Rufus,
Hippocrates, and Hali, and Galen,
Serapion, Rhazes, and Avicen,
Averrhoës, Gilbert, and Constantine,
Bernard, and Gatisden, and John Damascene.[35]
In diet he was measured as could be,
Including naught of superfluity,
But nourishing and easy. It's no libel
To say he read but little in the Bible.

33. *astronomy*] Chaucer means the "science" we would now call astrology.
34. *boot*] remedy, relief.
35. *Esculapius . . . John Damascene*] supposed and actual authors of medieval treatises on medicine.

In blue and scarlet he went clad, withal,
Lined with a taffeta and with sendal;
And yet he was right chary of expense;
He kept the gold he gained from pestilence.
For gold in physic is a fine cordial,
And therefore loved he gold exceeding all.

The Wife of Bath

There was a housewife come from Bath, or near,
Who — sad to say — was deaf in either ear.
At making cloth she had so great a bent
She bettered those of Ypres and even of Ghent.
In all the parish there was no goodwife
Should offering make before her, on my life;
And if one did, indeed, so wroth was she
It put her out of all her charity.
Her kerchiefs were of finest weave and ground;
I dare swear that they weighed a full ten pound
Which, of a Sunday, she wore on her head.
Her hose were of the choicest scarlet red,
Close gartered, and her shoes were soft and new.
Bold was her face, and fair, and red of hue.
She'd been respectable throughout her life,
With five churched husbands bringing joy and strife,
Not counting other company in youth;
But thereof there's no need to speak, in truth.
Three times she'd journeyed to Jerusalem;
And many a foreign stream she'd had to stem;
At Rome she'd been, and she'd been in Boulogne,
In Spain at Santiago, and at Cologne.
She could tell much of wandering by the way:
Gap-toothed was she, it is no lie to say.
Upon an ambler easily she sat,
Well wimpled, aye, and over all a hat
As broad as is a buckler or a targe;[36]
A rug was tucked around her buttocks large,

36. *buckler . . . targe*] small shields.

And on her feet a pair of sharpened spurs.
In company well could she laugh her slurs.
The remedies of love she knew, perchance,
For of that art she'd learned the old, old dance.

The Parson

There was a good man of religion, too,
A country parson, poor, I warrant you;
But rich he was in holy thought and work.
He was a learned man also, a clerk,
Who Christ's own gospel truly sought to preach;
Devoutly his parishioners would he teach.
Benign he was and wondrous diligent.
Patient in adverse times and well content,
As he was ofttimes proven; always blithe,
He was right loath to curse to get a tithe,
But rather would he give, in case of doubt,
Unto those poor parishioners about,
Part of his income, even of his goods.
Enough with little, coloured all his moods.
Wide was his parish, houses far asunder,
But never did he fail, for rain or thunder,
In sickness, or in sin, or any state,
To visit to the farthest, small and great,
Going afoot, and in his hand a stave.
This fine example to his flock he gave,
That first he wrought and afterwards he taught;
Out of the gospel then that text he caught,
And this figure he added thereunto —
That, if gold rust, what shall poor iron do?
For if the priest be foul, in whom we trust,
What wonder if a layman yield to lust?
And shame it is, if priest take thought for keep,
A shitty shepherd, shepherding clean sheep.
Well ought a priest example good to give,
By his own cleanness, how his flock should live.
He never let his benefice for hire,
Leaving his flock to flounder in the mire,
And ran to London, up to old Saint Paul's

To get himself a chantry there for souls,
Nor in some brotherhood did he withhold;
But dwelt at home and kept so well the fold
That never wolf could make his plans miscarry;
He was a shepherd and not mercenary.
And holy though he was, and virtuous,
To sinners he was not impiteous,
Nor haughty in his speech, nor too divine,
But in all teaching prudent and benign.
To lead folk into Heaven but by stress
Of good example was his busyness.
But if some sinful one proved obstinate,
Be who it might, of high or low estate,
Him he reproved, and sharply, as I know.
There is nowhere a better priest, I trow.
He had no thirst for pomp or reverence,
Nor made himself a special, spiced conscience,
But Christ's own lore, and His apostles' twelve
He taught, but first he followed it himselve.

The Plowman

With him there was a plowman, was his brother,
That many a load of dung, and many another
Had scattered, for a good true toiler, he,
Living in peace and perfect charity.
He loved God most, and that with his whole heart,
At all times, though he played or plied his art,
And next, his neighbour, even as himself.
He'd thresh and dig, with never thought of pelf,[37]
For Christ's own sake, for every poor wight,
All without pay, if it lay in his might.
He paid his taxes, fully, fairly, well,
Both by his own toil and by stuff he'd sell.
In a tabard[38] he rode upon a mare.
　　There were also a reeve[39] and miller there;

37. *pelf*] money, riches.
38. *tabard*] a short, loose-fitting sleeveless or short-sleeved coat or cape.
39. *reeve*] a steward or bailiff of an estate.

A summoner, manciple[40] and pardoner,
And these, beside myself, made all there were.

The Miller

The miller was a stout churl, be it known,
Hardy and big of brawn and big of bone;
Which was well proved, for when he went on lam
At wrestling, never failed he of the ram.[41]
He was a chunky fellow, broad of build;
He'd heave a door from hinges if he willed,
Or break it through, by running, with his head.
His beard, as any sow or fox, was red,
And broad it was as if it were a spade.
Upon the coping of his nose he had
A wart, and thereon stood a tuft of hairs,
Red as the bristles in an old sow's ears;
His nostrils they were black and very wide.
A sword and buckler bore he by his side.
His mouth was like a furnace door for size.
He was a jester and could poetize,
But mostly all of sin and ribaldries.
He could steal corn and full thrice charge his fees;
And yet he had a thumb of gold, begad.
A white coat and blue hood he wore, this lad.
A bagpipe he could blow well, be it known,
And with that same he brought us out of town.

The Manciple

There was a manciple from an inn of court,
To whom all buyers might quite well resort
To learn the art of buying food and drink;
For whether he paid cash or not, I think
That he so knew the markets, when to buy,

---

40. *summoner, manciple and pardoner*] a summoner served summonses to the ecclesiastical courts, a manciple was an officer who purchased victuals for a college and a pardoner dispensed papal pardons.
41. *ram*] a usual prize in wrestling.

He never found himself left high and dry.
Now is it not of God a full fair grace
That such a vulgar man has wit to pace
The wisdom of a crowd of learned men?
Of masters had he more than three times ten,
Who were in law expert and curious;
Whereof there were a dozen in that house
Fit to be stewards of both rent and land
Of any lord in England who would stand
Upon his own and live in manner good,
In honour, debtless (save his head were wood),
Or live as frugally as he might desire;
These men were able to have helped a shire
In any case that ever might befall;
And yet this manciple outguessed them all.

The Reeve

The reeve he was a slender, choleric man,
Who shaved his beard as close as razor can.
His hair was cut round even with his ears;
His top was tonsured like a pulpiteer's.
Long were his legs, and they were very lean,
And like a staff, with no calf to be seen.
Well could he manage granary and bin;
No auditor could ever on him win.
He could foretell, by drought and by the rain,
The yielding of his seed and of his grain.
His lord's sheep and his oxen and his dairy,
His swine and horses, all his stores, his poultry,
Were wholly in this steward's managing;
And, by agreement, he'd made reckoning
Since his young lord of age was twenty years;
Yet no man ever found him in arrears.
There was no agent, hind, or herd who'd cheat
But he knew well his cunning and deceit;
They were afraid of him as of the death.
His cottage was a good one, on a heath;
By green trees shaded with this dwelling-place.

Much better than his lord could he purchase.
Right rich he was in his own private right,
Seeing he'd pleased his lord, by day or night,
By giving him, or lending, of his goods,
And so got thanked — but yet got coats and hoods.
In youth he'd learned a good trade, and had been
A carpenter, as fine as could be seen.
This steward sat a horse that well could trot,
And was all dapple-grey, and was named Scot.
A long surcoat of blue did he parade,
And at his side he bore a rusty blade.
Of Norfolk was this reeve of whom I tell,
From near a town that men call Badeswell.
Bundled he was like friar from chin to croup,
And ever he rode hindmost of our troop.

The Summoner

A summoner was with us in that place,
Who had a fiery-red, cherubic face,
For eczema he had; his eyes were narrow.
As hot he was, and lecherous, as a sparrow;
With black and scabby brows and scanty beard;
He had a face that little children feared.
There was no mercury, sulphur, or litharge,
No borax, ceruse, tartar, could discharge,
Nor ointment that could cleanse enough, or bite,
To free him of his boils and pimples white,
Nor of the bosses resting on his cheeks.
Well loved he garlic, onions, aye and leeks,
And drinking of strong wine as red as blood.
Then would he talk and shout as madman would.
And when a deal of wine he'd poured within,
Then would he utter no word save Latin.
Some phrases had he learned, say two or three,
Which he had garnered out of some decree;
No wonder, for he'd heard it all the day;
And all you know right well that even a jay
Can call out "Wat" as well as can the pope.
But when, for aught else, into him you'd grope,

'Twas found he'd spent his whole philosophy;
Just "*Questio quid juris*"[42] would he cry.
He was a noble rascal, and a kind;
A better comrade 'twould be hard to find.
Why, he would suffer, for a quart of wine,
Some good fellow to have his concubine
A twelve-month, and excuse him to the full
(Between ourselves, though, he could pluck a gull).
And if he chanced upon a good fellow,
He would instruct him never to have awe,
In such a case, of the archdeacon's curse,
Except a man's soul lie within his purse;
For in his purse the man should punished be.
"The purse is the archdeacon's Hell," said he.
But well I know he lied in what he said;
A curse ought every guilty man to dread
(For curse can kill, as absolution save),
And 'ware *significavit*[43] to the grave.
In his own power had he, and at ease,
The boys and girls of all the diocese,
And knew their secrets, and by counsel led.
A garland had he set upon his head,
Large as a tavern's wine-bush on a stake;
A buckler had he made of bread they bake.

The Pardoner

With him there rode a gentle pardoner
Of Rouncival, his friend and his compeer;
Straight from the court of Rome had journeyed he.
Loudly he sang "Come hither, love, to me,"
The summoner joining with a burden round;
Was never horn of half so great a sound.
This pardoner had hair as yellow as wax,
But lank it hung as does a strike of flax;
In wisps hung down such locks as he'd on head,

42. "Questio quid juris"] "What point of law does this investigation involve?"
43. significavit] the writ that transferred someone found guilty in the ecclesiastical court
   to a civil court to administer punishment.

And with them he his shoulders overspread;
But thin they dropped, and stringy, one by one.
But as to hood, for sport of it, he'd none,
Though it was packed in wallet all the while.
It seemed to him he went in latest style,
Dishevelled, save for cap, his head all bare.
As shiny eyes he had as has a hare.
He had a fine veronica[44] sewed to cap.
His wallet lay before him in his lap,
Stuffed full of pardons brought from Rome all hot.
A voice he had that bleated like a goat.
No beard had he, nor ever should he have,
For smooth his face as he'd just had a shave;
I think he was a gelding or a mare.
But in his craft, from Berwick unto Ware,
Was no such pardoner in any place.
For in his bag he had a pillowcase
The which, he said, was Our True Lady's veil:
He said he had a piece of the very sail
That good Saint Peter had, what time he went
Upon the sea, till Jesus changed his bent.
He had a latten cross set full of stones,
And in a bottle had he some pig's bones.
But with these relics, when he came upon
Some simple parson, then this paragon
In that one day more money stood to gain
Than the poor dupe in two months could attain.
And thus, with flattery and suchlike japes,
He made the parson and the rest his apes.
But yet, to tell the whole truth at the last,
He was, in church, a fine ecclesiast.
Well could he read a lesson or a story,
But best of all he sang an offertory;
For well he knew that when that song was sung,
Then might he preach, and all with polished tongue,
To win some silver, as he right well could;
Therefore he sang so merrily and so loud.

Now have I told you briefly, in a clause,

---

44. *veronica*] portrait of Christ's face as it was reported to have been impressed on St. Veronica's handkerchief.

The state, the array, the number, and the cause
Of the assembling of this company
In Southwark, at this noble hostelry
Known as the Tabard Inn, hard by the Bell.
But now the time is come wherein to tell
How all we bore ourselves that very night
When at the hostelry we did alight.
And afterward the story I engage
To tell you of our common pilgrimage.
But first, I pray you, of your courtesy,
You'll not ascribe it to vulgarity
Though I speak plainly of this matter here,
Retailing you their words and means of cheer;
Nor though I use their very terms, nor lie.
For this thing do you know as well as I:
When one repeats a tale told by a man,
He must report, as nearly as he can,
Every least word, if he remember it,
However rude it be, or how unfit;
Or else he may be telling what's untrue,
Embellishing and fictionizing too.
He may not spare, although it were his brother;
He must as well say one word as another.
Christ spoke right broadly out, in holy writ,
And, you know well, there's nothing low in it.
And Plato says, to those able to read:
"The word should be the cousin to the deed."
Also, I pray that you'll forgive it me
If I have not set folk, in their degree
Here in this tale, by rank as they should stand.
My wits are not the best, you'll understand.

Great cheer our host gave to us, every one,
And to the supper set us all anon;
And served us then with victuals of the best.
Strong was the wine and pleasant to each guest.
A seemly man our good host was, withal,
Fit to have been a marshal in some hall;
He was a large man, with protruding eyes,
As fine a burgher as in Cheapside lies;
Bold in his speech, and wise, and right well taught,

And as to manhood, lacking there in naught.
Also, he was a very merry man,
And after meat, at playing he began,
Speaking of mirth among some other things,
When all of us had paid our reckonings;
And saying thus: "Now masters, verily
You are all welcome here, and heartily:
For by my truth, and telling you no lie,
I have not seen, this year, a company
Here in this inn, fitter for sport than now.
Fain would I make you happy, knew I how.
And of a game have I this moment thought
To give you joy, and it shall cost you naught.
    "You go to Canterbury; may God speed
And the blest martyr soon requite your meed.[45]
And well I know, as you go on your way,
You'll tell good tales and shape yourselves to play;
For truly there's no mirth nor comfort, none,
Riding the roads as dumb as is a stone;
And therefore will I furnish you a sport,
As I just said, to give you some comfort.
And if you like it, all, by one assent,
And will be ruled by me, of my judgment,
And will so do as I'll proceed to say,
Tomorrow, when you ride upon your way,
Then, by my father's spirit, who is dead,
If you're not gay, I'll give you up my head.
Hold up your hands, nor more about it speak."
    Our full assenting was not far to seek;
We thought there was no reason to think twice,
And granted him his way without advice,
And bade him tell his verdict just and wise,
    "Masters," quoth he, "here now is my advice;
But take it not, I pray you, in disdain;
This is the point, to put it short and plain,
That each of you, beguiling the long day,
Shall tell two stories as you wend your way
To Canterbury town; and each of you
On coming home, shall tell another two,

45. *meed*] reward.

All of adventures he has known befall.
And he who plays his part the best of all,
That is to say, who tells upon the road
Tales of best sense, in most amusing mode,
Shall have a supper at the others' cost
Here in this room and sitting by this post,
When we come back again from Canterbury.
And now, the more to warrant you'll be merry,
I will myself, and gladly, with you ride
At my own cost, and I will be your guide.
But whosoever shall my rule gainsay
Shall pay for all that's bought along the way.
And if you are agreed that it be so,
Tell me at once, or if not, tell me no,
And I will act accordingly. No more."

   This thing was granted, and our oaths we swore,
With right glad hearts, and prayed of him, also,
That he would take the office, nor forgo
The place of governor of all of us,
Judging our tales; and by his wisdom thus
Arrange that supper at a certain price,
We to be ruled, each one, by his advice
In things both great and small; by one assent,
We stood committed to his government.
And thereupon, the wine was fetched anon;
We drank, and then to rest went every one,
And that without a longer tarrying.

   Next morning, when the day began to spring,
Up rose our host, and acting as our cock,
He gathered us together in a flock,
And forth we rode, a jog-trot being the pace,
Until we reached Saint Thomas' watering-place.
And there our host pulled horse up to a walk,
And said: "Now, masters, listen while I talk.
You know what you agreed at set of sun.
If even-song and morning-song are one,
Let's here decide who first shall tell a tale.
And as I hope to drink more wine and ale,
Whoso proves rebel to my government
Shall pay for all that by the way is spent.
Come now, draw cuts, before we farther win,

And he that draws the shortest shall begin.
Sir knight," said he, "my master and my lord,
You shall draw first as you have pledged your word.
Come near," quoth he, "my lady prioress:
And you, sir clerk, put by your bashfulness,
Nor ponder more; out hands, now, every man!"

At once to draw a cut each one began,
And, to make short the matter, as it was,
Whether by chance or whatsoever cause,
The truth is, that the cut fell to the knight,
At which right happy then was every wight.
Thus that his story first of all he'd tell,
According to the compact, it befell,
As you have heard. Why argue to and fro?
And when this good man saw that it was so,
Being a wise man and obedient
To plighted word, given by free assent,
He said: "Since I must then begin the game,
Why, welcome be the cut, and in God's name!
Now let us ride, and hearken what I say."

And at that word we rode forth on our way;
And he began to speak, with right good cheer,
His tale anon, as it is written here.

HERE ENDS THE PROLOGUE OF THIS BOOK
AND HERE BEGINS THE FIRST TALE,
WHICH IS THE KNIGHT'S TALE

THE KNIGHT'S TALE

Iamque domos patrias, Scithice post aspera gentis Prelia, laurigero, etc.[1]
— STATIUS, *Theb.*, *XII, 519.*

ONCE ON A TIME, as old tales tell to us,
There was a duke whose name was Theseus;
Of Athens he was lord and governor,
And in his time was such a conqueror
That greater was there not beneath the sun.
Full many a rich country had he won;
What with his wisdom and his chivalry
He gained the realm of Femininity,
That was of old time known as Scythia.
There wedded he the queen, Hippolyta,
And brought her home with him to his country.
In glory great and with great pageantry,
And, too, her younger sister, Emily.
And thus, in victory and with melody,
Let I this noble duke to Athens ride
With all his armed host marching at his side.
    And truly, were it not too long to hear,
I would have told you fully how that year,
Was gained the realm of Femininity
By Theseus and by his chivalry;
And all of the great battle that was wrought
Where Amazons and the Athenians fought;
And how was wooed and won Hippolyta,
That fair and hardy queen of Scythia;
And of the feast was made at their wedding,
And of the tempest at their home-coming;
But all of that I must for now forbear.
I have, God knows, a large field for my share,
And weak the oxen, and the soil is tough.
The remnant of the tale is long enough.

1. *Iamque . . . etc.*] "And now to their native homes, after the rough wars against the
   Scythian tribe, with laurel-bearing. . . ."

I will not hinder any, in my turn;
Let each man tell his tale, until we learn
Which of us all the most deserves to win;
So where I stopped, again I'll now begin.
    This duke of whom I speak, of great renown,
When he had drawn almost unto the town,
In all well-being and in utmost pride,
He grew aware, casting his eyes aside,
That right upon the road, as suppliants do,
A company of ladies, two by two,
Knelt, all in black, before his cavalcade;
But such a clamorous cry of woe they made
That in the whole world living man had heard
No such a lamentation, on my word;
Nor would they cease lamenting till at last
They'd clutched his bridle reins and held them fast.
    "What folk are you that at my home-coming
Disturb my triumph with this dolorous thing?"
Cried Thesëus. "Do you so much envy
My honour that you thus complain and cry?
Or who has wronged you now, or who offended?
Come, tell me whether it may be amended;
And tell me, why are you clothed thus, in black?"
    The eldest lady of them answered back,
After she'd swooned, with cheek so deathly drear
That it was pitiful to see and hear,
And said: "Lord, to whom Fortune has but given
Victory, and to conquer where you've striven,
Your glory and your honour grieve not us;
But we beseech your aid and pity thus.
Have mercy on our woe and our distress.
Some drop of pity, of your gentleness,
Upon us wretched women, oh, let fall!
For see, lord, there is no one of us all
That has not been a duchess or a queen;
Now we are captives, as may well be seen:
Thanks be to Fortune and her treacherous wheel,
There's none can rest assured of constant weal.
And truly, lord, expecting your return,
In Pity's temple, where the fires yet burn,
We have been waiting through a long fortnight;

Now help us, lord, since it is in your might.
　"I, wretched woman, who am weeping thus,
Was once the wife of King Capanëus,
Who died at Thebes, oh, cursed be the day!
And all we that you see in this array,
And make this lamentation to be known,
All we have lost our husbands at that town
During the siege that round about it lay.
And now the old Creon, ah welaway!
The lord and governor of Thebes city,
Full of his wrath and all iniquity,
He, in despite and out of tyranny,
To do the dead a shame and villainy,
Of all our husbands, lying among the slain,
Has piled the bodies in a heap, amain,
And will not suffer them, nor give consent,
To buried be, or burned, nor will relent,
But sets his dogs to eat them, out of spite."
　And on that word, at once, without respite,
They all fell prone and cried out piteously:
"Have on us wretched women some mercy,
And let our sorrows sink into your heart!"
　This gentle duke down from his horse did start
With heart of pity, when he'd heard them speak.
It seemed to him his heart must surely break,
Seeing them there so miserable of state,
Who had been proud and happy but so late.
And in his arms he took them tenderly,
Giving them comfort understandingly:
And swore his oath, that as he was true knight,
He would put forth so thoroughly his might
Against the tyrant Creon as to wreak
Vengeance so great that all of Greece should speak
And say how Creon was by Thesëus served,
As one that had his death full well deserved.
This sworn and done, he no more there abode;
His banner he displayed and forth he rode
Toward Thebes, and all his host marched on beside;
Nor nearer Athens would he walk or ride,
Nor take his ease for even half a day,
But onward, and in camp that night he lay;

And thence he sent Hippolyta the queen
And her bright sister Emily, I ween,
Unto the town of Athens, there to dwell
While he went forth. There is no more to tell.
    The image of red Mars, with spear and shield,
So shone upon his banner's snow-white field
It made a billowing glitter up and down;
And by the banner borne was his pennon,
On which in beaten gold was worked, complete,
The Minotaur, which he had slain in Crete.
Thus rode this duke, thus rode this conqueror,
And in his host of chivalry the flower,
Until he came to Thebes and did alight
Full in the field where he'd intent to fight.
But to be brief in telling of this thing,
With Creon, who was Thebes' dread lord and king,
He fought and slew him, manfully, like knight,
In open war, and put his host to flight;
And by assault he took the city then,
Levelling wall and rafter with his men;
And to the ladies he restored again
The bones of their poor husbands who were slain,
To do for them the last rites of that day.
But it were far too long a tale to say
The clamour of great grief and sorrowing
Those ladies raised above the bones burning
Upon the pyres, and of the great honour
That Theseüs, the noble conqueror,
Paid to the ladies when from him they went;
To make the story short is my intent.
When, then, this worthy duke, this Theseüs
Had slain Creon and won Thebes city thus,
Still on the field he took that night his rest,
And dealt with all the land as he thought best.
    In searching through the heap of enemy dead,
Stripping them of their gear from heel to head,
The busy pillagers could pick and choose,
After the battle, what they best could use;
And so befell that in a heap they found,
Pierced through with many a grievous, bloody wound,
Two young knights lying together, side by side,

Bearing one crest, wrought richly, of their pride,
And of those two Arcita was the one,
The other knight was known as Palamon.
Not fully quick, nor fully dead they were,
But by their coats of arms and by their gear
The heralds readily could tell, withal,
That they were of the Theban blood royal,
And that they had been of two sisters born.
Out of the heap the spoilers had them torn
And carried gently over to the tent
Of Theseus; who shortly had them sent
To Athens, there in prison cell to lie
For ever, without ransom, till they die.
And when this worthy duke had all this done,
He gathered host and home he rode anon,
With laurel crowned again as conqueror;
There lived he in all joy and all honour
His term of life; what more need words express?
And in a tower, in anguish and distress,
Palamon and Arcita, day and night,
Dwelt whence no gold might help them to take flight.
  Thus passed by year by year and day by day,
Till it fell out, upon a morn in May,
That Emily, far fairer to be seen
Than is the lily on its stalk of green,
And fresher than is May with flowers new
(For with the rose's colour strove her hue,
I know not which was fairer of the two),
Before the dawn, as was her wont to do,
She rose and dressed her body for delight;
For May will have no sluggards of the night.
That season rouses every gentle heart
And forces it from winter's sleep to start,
Saying: "Arise and show thy reverence."
So Emily remembered to go thence
In honour of the May, and so she rose.
Clothed, she was sweeter than any flower that blows;
Her yellow hair was braided in one tress
Behind her back, a full yard long, I guess.
And in the garden, as the sun up-rose,
She sauntered back and forth and through each close,

Gathering many a flower, white and red,
To weave a delicate garland for her head;
And like a heavenly angel's was her song.
The tower tall, which was so thick and strong,
And of the castle was the great donjon,
(Wherein the two knights languished in prison,
Of whom I told and shall yet tell, withal),
Was joined, at base, unto the garden wall
Whereunder Emily went dallying.
Bright was the sun and clear that morn in spring,
And Palamon, the woeful prisoner,
As was his wont, by leave of his gaoler,
Was up and pacing round that chamber high,
From which the noble city filled his eye,
And, too, the garden full of branches green,
Wherein bright Emily, fair and serene,
Went walking and went roving up and down.
This sorrowing prisoner, this Palamon,
Being in the chamber, pacing to and fro,
And to himself complaining of his woe,
Cursing his birth, he often cried "Alas!"
And so it was, by chance or other pass,
That through a window, closed by many a bar
Of iron, strong and square as any spar,
He cast his eyes upon Emilia,
And thereupon he blenched[2] and cried out "Ah!"
As if he had been smitten to the heart.
And at that cry Arcita did up-start,
Asking: "My cousin, why what ails you now
That you've so deathly pallor on your brow?
Why did you cry out? Who's offended you?
For God's love, show some patience, as I do,
With prison, for it may not different be;
Fortune has given this adversity.
Some evil disposition or aspect
Of Saturn did our horoscopes affect
To bring us here, though differently 'twere sworn;
But so the stars stood when we two were born;
We must endure it; that, in brief, is plain."
    This Palamon replied and said again:

---

2. *blenched*] blanched, turned pale.

"Cousin, indeed in this opinion now
Your fancy is but vanity, I trow.
It's not our prison that caused me to cry.
But I was wounded lately through the eye
Down to my heart, and that my bane will be.
The beauty of the lady that I see
There in that garden, pacing to and fro,
Is cause of all my crying and my woe.
I know not if she's woman or goddess;
But Venus she is verily, I guess."
And thereupon down on his knees he fell,
And said: "O Venus, if it be thy will
To be transfigured in this garden, thus
Before me, sorrowing wretch, oh now help us
Out of this prison to be soon escaped.
And if it be my destiny is shaped,
By fate, to die in durance, in bondage,
Have pity, then, upon our lineage
That has been brought so low by tyranny."
    And on that word Arcita looked to see
This lady who went roving to and fro.
And in that look her beauty struck him so
That, if poor Palamon is wounded sore,
Arcita is as deeply hurt, and more.
And with a sigh he said then, piteously:
"The virgin beauty slays me suddenly
Of her that wanders yonder in that place;
And save I have her pity and her grace,
That I at least may see her day by day,
I am but dead; there is no more to say."
    This Palamon, when these words he had heard,
Pitilessly he watched him, and answered:
"Do you say this in earnest or in play?"
    "Nay," quoth Arcita, "earnest, now, I say!
God help me, I am in no mood for play!"
    Palamon knit his brows and stood at bay.
"It will not prove," he said, "to your honour
After so long a time to turn traitor
To me, who am your cousin and your brother,
Sworn as we are, and each unto the other,
That never, though for death in any pain,
Never, indeed, till death shall part us twain,

Either of us in love shall hinder other,
No, nor in any thing, O my dear brother;
But that, instead, you shall so further me
As I shall you. All this we did agree.
Such was your oath and such was mine also.
You dare not now deny it, well I know.
Thus you are of my party, beyond doubt.
And now you would all falsely go about
To love my lady, whom I love and serve,
And shall while life my heart's blood may preserve.
Nay, false Arcita, it shall not be so.
I loved her first, and told you all my woe,
As to a brother and to one that swore
To further me, as I have said before.
For which you are in duty bound, as knight,
To help me, if the thing lie in your might,
Or else you're false, I say, and downfallen."
    Then this Arcita proudly spoke again:
"You shall," he said, "be rather false than I;
And that you're so, I tell you utterly;
For *par amour* I loved her first, you know.
What can you say? You know not, even now,
Whether she is a woman or goddess!
Yours is a worship as of holiness,
While mine is love, as of a mortal maid;
Wherefore I told you of it, unafraid,
As to my cousin and my brother sworn.
Let us assume you loved her first, this morn;
Know you not well the ancient writer's saw
Of 'Who shall give a lover any law?'
Love is a greater law, aye by my pan,[3]
Than man has ever given to earthly man.
And therefore statute law and such decrees
Are broken daily and in all degrees.
A man must needs have love, maugre his head.
He cannot flee it though he should be dead,
And be she maid, or widow, or a wife.
And yet it is not likely that, in life,
You'll stand within her graces; nor shall I;
For you are well aware, aye verily,

3. *pan*] the brain-pan; the skull.

That you and I are doomed to prison drear
Perpetually; we gain no ransom here.
We strive but as those dogs did for the bone;
They fought all day, and yet their gain was none.
Till came a kite while they were still so wroth
And bore the bone away between them both.
And therefore, at the king's court, O my brother,
It's each man for himself and not for other.
Love if you like; for I love and aye shall;
And certainly, dear brother, that is all.
Here in this prison cell must we remain
And each endure whatever fate ordain."
 Great was the strife, and long, betwixt the two,
If I had but the time to tell it you,
Save in effect. It happened on a day
(To tell the tale as briefly as I may),
A worthy duke men called Pirithous,
Who had been friend unto Duke Thesëus,
Since each had been a little child, a chit,
Was come to visit Athens and visit
His play-fellow, as he was wont to do,
For in this whole world he loved no man so;
And Thesëus loved him as truly — nay,
So well each loved the other, old books say,
That when one died (it is but truth I tell),
The other went and sought him down in Hell;
But of that tale I have no wish to write.
Pirithous loved Arcita, too, that knight,
Having known him in Thebes full many a year;
And finally, at his request and prayer,
And that without a coin of ransom paid,
Duke Thesëus released him out of shade,
Freely to go where'er he wished, and to
His own devices, as I'll now tell you.
 The compact was, to set it plainly down,
As made between those two of great renown:
That if Arcita, any time, were found,
Ever in life, by day or night, on ground
Of any country of this Thesëus,
And he were caught, it was concerted thus,
That by the sword he straight should lose his head.
He had no choice, so taking leave he sped

Homeward to Thebes, lest by the sword's sharp edge
He forfeit life. His neck was under pledge.
　　How great a sorrow is Arcita's now!
How through his heart he feels death's heavy blow;
He weeps, he wails, he cries out piteously;
He thinks to slay himself all privily.
Said he: "Alas, the day that I was born!
I'm in worse prison, now, and more forlorn;
Now am I doomed eternally to dwell
No more in Purgatory, but in Hell.
Alas, that I have known Pirithoüs!
For else had I remained with Theseüs,
Fettered within that cell; but even so
Then had I been in bliss and not in woe.
Only the sight of her that I would serve,
Though I might never her dear grace deserve,
Would have sufficed, oh well enough for me!
O my dear cousin Palamon," said he,
"Yours is the victory, and that is sure,
For there, full happily, you may endure.
In prison? Never, but in Paradise!
Oh, well has Fortune turned for you the dice,
Who have the sight of her, I the absence.
For possible it is, in her presence,
You being a knight, a worthy and able,
That by some chance, since Fortune's changeable,
You may to your desire sometime attain.
But I, that am in exile and in pain,
Stripped of all hope and in so deep despair
That there's no earth nor water, fire nor air,
Nor any creature made of them there is
To help or give me comfort, now, in this —
Surely I'll die of sorrow and distress;
Farewell, my life, my love, my joyousness!
　　"Alas! Why is it men so much complain
Of what great God, or Fortune, may ordain,
When better is the gift, in any guise,
Than men may often for themselves devise?
One man desires only that great wealth
Which may but cause his death or long ill-health.
One who from prison gladly would be free,

At home by his own servants slain might be.
Infinite evils lie therein, 'tis clear;
We know not what it is we pray for here.
We fare as he that's drunken as a mouse;
A drunk man knows right well he has a house,
But he knows not the right way leading thither;
And a drunk man is sure to slip and slither.
And certainly, in this world so fare we;
We furiously pursue felicity,
Yet we go often wrong before we die.
This may we all admit, and specially I,
Who deemed and held, as I were under spell,
That if I might escape from prison cell,
Then would I find again what joy might heal,
Who now am only exiled from my weal.
For since I may not see you, Emily,
I am but dead; there is no remedy."

   And on the other hand, this Palamon,
When that he found Arcita truly gone,
Such lamentation made he, that the tower
Resounded of his crying, hour by hour.
The very fetters on his legs were yet
Again with all his bitter salt tears wet.
"Alas!" said he, "Arcita, cousin mine,
With all our strife, God knows, you've won the wine.
You're walking, now, in Theban streets, at large,
And all my woe you may from mind discharge.
You may, too, since you've wisdom and manhood,
Assemble all the people of our blood
And wage a war so sharp on this city
That by some fortune, or by some treaty,
You shall yet have that lady to your wife
For whom I now must needs lay down my life.
For surely 'tis in possibility,
Since you are now at large, from prison free,
And are a lord, great is your advantage
Above my own, who die here in a cage.
For I must weep and wail, the while I live,
In all the grief that prison cell may give,
And now with pain that love gives me, also,
Which doubles all my torment and my woe."

Therewith the fires of jealousy up-start
Within his breast and burn him to the heart
So wildly that he seems one, to behold,
Like seared box tree, or ashes, dead and cold.
Then said he: "O you cruel Gods, that sway
This world in bondage of your laws, for aye,
And write upon the tablets adamant
Your counsels and the changeless words you grant,
What better view of mankind do you hold
Than of the sheep that huddle in the fold?
For man must die like any other beast,
Or rot in prison, under foul arrest,
And suffer sickness and misfortune sad,
And still be ofttimes guiltless, too, by gad!

"What management is in this prescience
That, guiltless, yet torments our innocence?
And this increases all my pain, as well,
That man is bound by law, nor may rebel,
For fear of God, but must repress his will,
Whereas a beast may all his lust fulfill.
And when a beast is dead, he feels no pain;
But, after death, man yet must weep amain,
Though in this world he had but care and woe:
There is no doubt that it is even so.
The answer leave I to divines to tell,
But well I know this present world is hell.
Alas! I see a serpent or a thief,
That has brought many a true man unto grief,
Going at large, and where he wills may turn,
But I must lie in gaol, because Saturn,
And Juno too, both envious and mad,
Have spilled out well-nigh all the blood we had
At Thebes, and desolated her wide walls.
And Venus slays me with the bitter galls
Of fear of Arcita, and jealousy."

Now will I leave this Palamon, for he
Is in his prison, where he still must dwell,
And of Arcita will I forthwith tell.

Summer being passed away and nights grown long,
Increased now doubly all the anguish strong
Both of the lover and the prisoner.

I know not which one was the woefuller.
For, to be brief about it, Palamon
Is doomed to lie for ever in prison,
In chains and fetters till he shall be dead;
And exiled (on the forfeit of his head)
Arcita must remain abroad, nor see,
For evermore, the face of his lady.
    You lovers, now I ask you this question:
Who has the worse, Arcita or Palamon?
The one may see his lady day by day,
But yet in prison must he dwell for aye.
The other, where he wishes, he may go,
But never see his lady more, ah no.
Now answer as you wish, all you that can,
For I will speak right on as I began.

> *Explicit prima pars.*
> *Sequitur pars secunda.*[4]

Now when Arcita unto Thebes was come,
He lay and languished all day in his home,
Since he his lady nevermore should see,
But telling of his sorrow brief I'll be.
Had never any man so much torture,
No, nor shall have while this world may endure.
Bereft he was of sleep and meat and drink,
That lean he grew and dry as shaft, I think.
His eyes were hollow and ghastly to behold,
His face was sallow, all pale and ashen-cold,
And solitary kept he and alone,
Wailing the whole night long, making his moan.
And if he heard a song or instrument,
Then he would weep ungoverned and lament;
So feeble were his spirits, and so low,
And so changed was he, that no man could know
Him by his words or voice, whoever heard.
And in this change, for all the world he fared
As if not troubled by malady of love,
But by that humor dark and grim, whereof
Springs melancholy madness in the brain,

---

4. Explicit . . . secunda] "The first part ends here. The second part follows."

And fantasy unbridled holds its reign.
And shortly, all was turned quite upside-down,
Both habits and the temper all had known
Of him, this woeful lover, Dan Arcite.
    Why should I all day of his woe indite?
When he'd endured all this a year or two,
This cruel torment and this pain and woe,
At Thebes, in his own country, as I said,
Upon a night, while sleeping in his bed,
He dreamed of how the winged God Mercury
Before him stood and bade him happier be.
His sleep-bestowing wand he bore upright;
A hat he wore upon his ringlets bright.
Arrayed this god was (noted at a leap)
As he'd been when to Argus he gave sleep.
And thus he spoke: "To Athens shall you wend;
For all your woe is destined there to end."
And on that word Arcita woke and started.
"Now truly, howsoever sore I'm smarted,"
Said he, "to Athens right now will I fare;
Nor for the dread of death will I now spare
To see my lady, whom I love and serve;
I will not reck of death, with her, nor swerve."
    And with that word he caught a great mirror,
And saw how changed was all his old colour,
And saw his visage altered from its kind.
And right away it ran into his mind
That since his face was now disfigured so,
By suffering endured (as well we know),
He might, if he should bear him low in town,
Live there in Athens evermore, unknown,
Seeing his lady well-nigh every day.
And right anon he altered his array,
Like a poor labourer in mean attire,
And all alone, save only for a squire,
Who knew his secret heart and all his case,
And who was dressed as poorly as he was,
To Athens was he gone the nearest way.
And to the court he went upon a day,
And at the gate he proffered services
To drudge and drag, as any one devises.

And to be brief herein, and to be plain,
He found employment with a chamberlain
Was serving in the house of Emily;
For he was sharp and very soon could see
What every servant did who served her there.
Right well could he hew wood and water bear,
For he was young and mighty, let me own,
And big of muscle, aye and big of bone,
To do what any man asked, in a trice.
A year or two he was in this service,
Page of the chamber of Emily the bright;
He said "Philostrates" would name him right.
But half so well beloved a man as he
Was never in that court, of his degree;
His gentle nature was so clearly shown,
That throughout all the court spread his renown.
They said it were but kindly courtesy
If Theseus should heighten his degree
And put him in more honourable service
Wherein he might his virtue exercise.
And thus, anon, his name was so up-sprung,
Both for his deeds and sayings of his tongue,
That Theseus had brought him nigh and nigher
And of the chamber he had made him squire,
And given him gold to maintain dignity.
Besides, men brought him, from his own country,
From year to year, clandestinely, his rent;
But honestly and slyly it was spent,
And no man wondered how he came by it.
And three years thus he lived, with much profit,
And bore him so in peace and so in war
There was no man that Theseus loved more.
And in such bliss I leave Arcita now,
And upon Palamon some words bestow.

   In darksome, horrible, and strong prison
These seven years has now sat Palamon,
Wasted by woe and by his long distress.
Who has a two-fold evil heaviness
But Palamon? whom love yet tortures so
That half out of his wits he is for woe;
And joined thereto he is a prisoner,

Perpetually, not only for a year.
And who could rhyme in English, properly,
His martyrdom? Forsooth, it is not I;
And therefore I pass lightly on my way.
  It fell out in the seventh year, in May,
On the third night (as say the books of old
Which have this story much more fully told),
Were it by chance or were it destiny
(Since, when a thing is destined, it must be),
That, shortly after midnight, Palamon,
By helping of a friend, broke from prison,
And fled the city, fast as he might go;
For he had given his guard a drink that so
Was mixed of spice and honey and certain wine
And Theban opiate and anodyne,
That all that night, although a man might shake
This gaoler, he slept on, nor could awake.
And thus he flees as fast as ever he may.
The night was short and it was nearly day,
Wherefore he needs must find a place to hide;
And to a grove that grew hard by, with stride
Of furtive foot, went fearful Palamon.
In brief, he'd formed his plan, as he went on,
That in the grove he would lie fast all day,
And when night came, then would he take his way
Toward Thebes, and there find friends, and of them pray
Their help on Thesëus in war's array;
And briefly either he would lose his life,
Or else win Emily to be his wife;
This is the gist of his intention plain.
  Now I'll return to Arcita again,
Who little knew how near to him was care
Till Fortune caught him in her tangling snare.
  The busy lark, the herald of the day,
Salutes now in her song the morning grey;
And fiery Phoebus rises up so bright
That all the east is laughing with the light,
And with his streamers dries, among the greves,[5]
The silver droplets hanging on the leaves.

5. *greves*] groves.

And so Arcita, in the court royal
With Theseüs, and his squire principal,
Is risen, and looks on the merry day.
And now, to do his reverence to May,
Calling to mind the point of his desire,
He on a courser, leaping high like fire,
Is ridden to the fields to muse and play,
Out of the court, a mile or two away;
And to the grove, whereof I lately told,
By accident his way began to hold,
To make him there the garland that one weaves
Of woodbine leaves and of green hawthorn leaves.
And loud he sang within the sunlit sheen:
"O May, with all thy flowers and all thy green,
Welcome be thou, thou fair and freshening May:
I hope to pluck some garland green today."
And from his courser, with a lusty heart,
Into the grove right hastily did start,
And on a path he wandered up and down,
Near which, and as it chanced, this Palamon
Lay in the thicket, where no man might see,
For sore afraid of finding death was he.
He knew not that Arcita was so near:
God knows he would have doubted eye and ear,
But it has been a truth these many years
That "Fields have eyes and every wood has ears."
It's well for one to bear himself with poise;
For every day unlooked-for chance annoys.
And little knew Arcita of his friend,
Who was so near and heard him to the end,
Where in the bush he sat now, keeping still.
    Arcita, having roamed and roved his fill,
And having sung his rondel, lustily,
Into a study fell he, suddenly,
As do these lovers in their strange desires,
Now in the trees, now down among the briers,
Now up, now down, like bucket in a well.
Even as on a Friday, truth to tell,
The sun shines now, and now the rain comes fast,
Even so can fickle Venus overcast
The spirits of her people; as her day

Is changeful, so she changes her array.
Seldom is Friday quite like all the week.
. Arcita, having sung, began to speak,
And sat him down, sighing like one forlorn.
"Alas," said he, "the day that I was born!
How long, O Juno, of thy cruelty,
Wilt thou wage bitter war on Thebes city?
Alas! Confounded beyond all reason
The blood of Cadmus and of Amphion;
Of royal Cadmus, who was the first man
To build at Thebes, and first the town began,
And first of all the city to be king;
Of his lineage am I, and his offspring,
By true descent, and of the stock royal:
And now I'm such a wretched serving thrall,
That he who is my mortal enemy,
I serve him as his squire, and all humbly.
And even more does Juno give me shame,
For I dare not acknowledge my own name;
But whereas I was Arcita by right,
Now I'm Philostrates, not worth a mite.
Alas, thou cruel Mars! Alas, Juno!
Thus have your angers all our kin brought low,
Save only me, and wretched Palamon,
Whom Thesëus martyrs yonder in prison.
And above all, to slay me utterly,
Love has his fiery dart so burningly
Struck through my faithful and care-laden heart,
My death was patterned ere my swaddling-shirt.
You slay me with your two eyes, Emily;
You are the cause for which I now must die.
For on the whole of all my other care
I would not set the value of a tare,
So I could do one thing to your pleasance!"
And with that word he fell down in a trance
That lasted long; and then he did up-start.
  This Palamon, who thought that through his heart
He felt a cold and sudden sword blade glide,
For rage he shook, no longer would he hide.
But after he had heard Arcita's tale,
As he were mad, with face gone deathly pale,

He started up and sprang out of the thicket,
Crying: "Arcita, oh you traitor wicked,
Now are you caught, that crave my lady so,
For whom I suffer all this pain and woe,
And are my blood, and know my secrets' store,
As I have often told you heretofore,
And have befooled the great Duke Theseüs,
And falsely changed your name and station thus:
Either I shall be dead or you shall die.
You shall not love my lady Emily,
But I will love her, and none other, no;
For I am Palamon, your mortal foe.
And though I have no weapon in this place,
Being but out of prison by God's grace,
I say again, that either you shall die
Or else forgo your love for Emily.
Choose which you will, for you shall not depart."
    This Arcita, with scornful, angry heart,
When he knew him and all the tale had heard,
Fierce as a lion, out he pulled a sword,
And answered thus: "By God that sits above!
Were it not you are sick and mad for love,
And that you have no weapon in this place,
Out of this grove you'd never move a pace,
But meet your death right now, and at my hand.
For I renounce the bond and its demand
Which you assert that I have made with you.
What, arrant fool, love's free to choose and do,
And I will have her, spite of all your might!
But in as much as you're a worthy knight
And willing to defend your love, in mail,
Hear now this word: tomorrow I'll not fail
(Without the cognizance of any wight)
To come here armed and harnessed as a knight,
And to bring arms for you, too, as you'll see;
And choose the better and leave the worse for me.
And meat and drink this very night I'll bring,
Enough for you, and clothes for your bedding.
And if it be that you my lady win
And slay me in this wood that now I'm in,
Then may you have your lady, for all of me."

This Palamon replied: "I do agree."
And thus they parted till the morrow morn,
When each had pledged his honour to return.
O Cupido, that know'st not charity!
O despot, that no peer will have with thee!
Truly, 'tis said, that love, like all lordship,
Declines, with little thanks, a partnership.
Well learned they that, Arcite and Palamon.
Arcita rode into the town anon,
And on the morrow, ere the dawn, he bore,
Secretly, arms and armour out of store,
Enough for each, and proper to maintain·
A battle in the field between the twain.
So on his horse, alone as he was born,
He carried out that harness as he'd sworn;
And in the grove, at time and place they'd set,
Arcita and this Palamon were met.
Each of the two changed colour in the face.
For as the hunter in the realm of Thrace
Stands at the clearing with his ready spear,
When hunted is the lion, or the bear,
And through the forest hears him rushing fast,
Breaking the boughs and leaves, and thinks aghast,
"Here comes apace my mortal enemy!
Now, without fail, he must be slain, or I;
For either I must kill him ere he pass,
Or he will make of me a dead carcass" —
So fared these men, in altering their hue,
So far as each the strength of other knew.
There was no "good-day" given, no saluting,
But without word, rehearsal, or such thing,
Each of them helping, so they armed each other
As dutifully as he were his own brother;
And afterward, with their sharp spears and strong,
They thrust each at the other wondrous long.
You might have fancied that this Palamon,
In battle, was a furious, mad lion,
And that Arcita was a tiger quite:
Like very boars the two began to smite,
Like boars that froth for anger in the wood.
Up to the ankles fought they in their blood.

And leaving them thus fighting fast and fell,
Forthwith of Theseus I now will tell.
  Great destiny, minister-general,
That executes in this world, and for all,
The needs that God foresaw ere we were born,
So strong it is that, though the world had sworn
The contrary of a thing, by yea or nay,
Yet sometime it shall fall upon a day,
Though not again within a thousand years.
For certainly our wishes and our fears,
Whether of war or peace, or hate or love,
All, all are ruled by that Foresight above.
This show I now by mighty Theseus,
Who to go hunting is so desirous,
And specially of the hart of ten, in May,
That, in his bed, there dawns for him no day
That he's not clothed and soon prepared to ride
With hound and horn and huntsman at his side.
For in his hunting has he such delight,
That it is all his joy and appetite
To be himself the great hart's deadly bane:
For after Mars, he serves Diana's reign.
  Clear was the day, as I have told ere this,
When Theseus, compact of joy and bliss,
With his Hippolyta, the lovely queen,
And fair Emilia, clothed all in green,
A-hunting they went riding royally.
And to the grove of trees that grew hard by,
In which there was a hart, as men had told,
Duke Theseus the shortest way did hold.
And to the glade he rode on, straight and right,
For there the hart was wont to go in flight,
And over a brook, and so forth on his way.
This duke would have a course at him today,
With such hounds as it pleased him to command.
  And when this duke was come upon that land,
Under the slanting sun he looked, anon,
And there saw Arcita and Palamon,
Who furiously fought, as two boars do;
The bright swords went in circles to and fro
So terribly, that even their least stroke

Seemed powerful enough to fell an oak;
But who the two were, nothing did he note.
This duke his courser with the sharp spurs smote,
And in one bound he was between the two,
And lugged his great sword out, and cried out: "Ho!
No more, I say, on pain of losing head!
By mighty Mars, that one shall soon be dead
Who smites another stroke that I may see!
But tell me now what manner of men ye be
That are so hardy as to fight out here
Without a judge or other officer,
As if you rode in lists right royally?"
    This Palamon replied, then, hastily,
Saying: "O Sire, what need for more ado?
We have deserved our death at hands of you.
Two woeful wretches are we, two captives
That are encumbered by our own sad lives;
And as you are a righteous lord and judge,
Give us not either mercy or refuge,
But slay me first, for sacred charity;
But slay my fellow here, as well, with me.
Or slay him first; for though you learn it late,
This is your mortal foe, Arcita — wait! —
That from the land was banished, on his head.
And for the which he merits to be dead.
For this is he who came unto your gate,
Calling himself Philostrates — nay, wait! —
Thus has he fooled you well this many a year,
And you have made him your chief squire, I hear:
And this is he that loves fair Emily.
For since the day is come when I must die,
I make confession plainly and say on,
That I am that same woeful Palamon
Who has your prison broken, viciously.
I am your mortal foe, and it is I
Who love so hotly Emily the bright
That I'll die gladly here within her sight.
Therefore do I ask death as penalty;
But slay my fellow with the same mercy,
For both of us deserve but to be slain."
    This worthy duke presently spoke again,

Saying: "This judgment needs but a short session:
Your own mouth, aye, and by your own confession,
Has doomed and damned you, as I shall record.
There is no need for torture, on my word.
But you shall die, by mighty Mars the red!"
    But then the queen, whose heart for pity bled,
Began to weep, and so did Emily
And all the ladies in the company.
Great pity must it be, so thought they all,
That ever such misfortune should befall:
For these were gentlemen, of great estate,
And for no thing, save love, was their debate.
They saw their bloody wounds, so sore and wide,
And all cried out—greater and less, they cried:
"Have mercy, lord, upon us women all!"
And down upon their bare knees did they fall,
And would have kissed his feet there where he stood,
Till at the last assuaged was his high mood;
For soon will pity flow through gentle heart.
And though he first for ire did shake and start,
He soon considered, to state the case in brief,
What cause they had for fighting, what for grief;
And though his anger still their guilt accused,
Yet in his reason he held them both excused;
In such wise: he thought well that every man
Will help himself in love, if he but can,
And will himself deliver from prison;
And, too, at heart he had compassion on
Those women, for they cried and wept as one;
And in his gentle heart he thought anon,
And softly to himself he said then: "Fie
Upon a lord that will have no mercy,
But acts the lion, both in word and deed,
To those repentant and in fear and need,
As well as to the proud and pitiless man
That still would do the thing that he began!
That lord must surely in discretion lack
Who, in such case, can no distinction make,
But weighs both proud and humble in one scale."
And shortly, when his ire was thus grown pale,
He looked up to the sky, with eyes alight,

And spoke these words, as he would promise plight:
"The god of love, ah *benedicite!*
How mighty and how great a lord is he!
Against his might may stand no obstacles,
A true god is he by his miracles;
For he can manage, in his own sweet wise,
The heart of anyone as he devise.
Lo, here, Arcita and this Palamon,
That were delivered out of my prison,
And might have lived in Thebes right royally,
Knowing me for their mortal enemy,
And also that their lives lay in my hand;
And yet their love has wiled them to this land,
Against all sense, and brought them here to die!
Look you now, is not that a folly high?
Who can be called a fool, except he love?
And see, for sake of God who sits above,
See how they bleed! Are they not well arrayed?
Thus has their lord, the god of love, repaid
Their wages and their fees for their service!
And yet they are supposed to be full wise
Who serve love well, whatever may befall!
But this is yet the best jest of them all,
That she for whom they have this jollity
Can thank them for it quite as much as me;
She knows no more of all this fervent fare,
By God! than knows a cuckoo or a hare.
But all must be essayed, both hot and cold,
A man must play the fool, when young or old;
I know it of myself from years long gone:
For of love's servants I've been numbered one.
And therefore, since I know well all love's pain,
And know how sorely it can man constrain,
As one that has been taken in the net,
I will forgive your trespass, and forget,
At instance of my sweet queen, kneeling here,
Aye, and of Emily, my sister dear.
And you shall presently consent to swear
That nevermore will you my power dare,
Nor wage war on me, either night or day,
But will be friends to me in all you may;

I do forgive this trespass, full and fair."
    And then they swore what he demanded there,
And, of his might, they of his mercy prayed,
And he extended grace, and thus he said:
"To speak for royalty's inheritress,
Although she be a queen or a princess,
Each of you both is worthy, I confess,
When comes the time to wed: but nonetheless,
I speak now of my sister Emily,
The cause of all this strife and jealousy —
You know yourselves she may not marry two,
At once, although you fight or what you do:
One of you, then, and be he loath or lief,
Must pipe his sorrows in an ivy leaf.
That is to say, she cannot have you both,
However jealous one may be, or wroth.
Therefore I put you both in this decree,
That each of you shall learn his destiny
As it is cast; and hear, now, in what wise
The word of fate shall speak through my device.
    "My will is this: to draw conclusion flat,
Without reply, or plea, or caveat
(In any case, accept it for the best),
That each of you shall follow his own quest,
Free of all ransom or of fear from me;
And this day, fifty weeks hence, both shall be
Here once again, each with a hundred knights,
Armed for the lists, who stoutly for your rights
Will ready be to battle, to maintain
Your claim to love. I promise you, again,
Upon my word, and as I am a knight,
That whichsoever of you wins the fight,
That is to say, whichever of you two
May with his hundred, whom I spoke of, do
His foe to death, or out of boundary drive,
Then he shall have Emilia to wive
To whom Fortuna gives so fair a grace.
The lists shall be erected in this place.
And God so truly on my soul have ruth
As I shall prove an honest judge, in truth.
You shall no other judgment in me waken

Than that the one shall die or else be taken.
And if you think the sentence is well said,
Speak your opinion, that you're well repaid.
This is the end, and I conclude hereon."
  Who looks up lightly now but Palamon?
Who leaps for you but Arcita the knight?
And who could tell, or who could ever write
The jubilation made within that place
Where Thesëus has shown so fair a grace?
But down on knee went each one for delight
And thanked him there with all his heart and might,
And specially those Thebans did their part.
And thus, with high hopes, being blithe of heart,
They took their leave; and homeward did they ride
To Thebes that sits within her old walls wide.

Explicit secunda pars.
Sequitur pars tercia.[6]

I think that men would deem it negligence
If I forgot to tell of the expense
Of Thesëus, who went so busily
To work upon the lists, right royally;
For such an amphitheatre he made,
Its equal never yet on earth was laid.
The circuit, rising, hemmed a mile about,
Walled all of stone and moated deep without.
Round was the shape as compass ever traces,
And built in tiers, the height of sixty paces,
That those who sat in one tier, or degree,
Should hinder not the folk behind to see.
  Eastward there stood a gate of marble white,
And westward such another, opposite.
In brief, no place on earth, and so sublime,
Was ever made in so small space of time;
For in the land there was no craftsman quick
At plane geometry or arithmetic,
No painter and no sculptor of hard stone,
But Thesëus pressed meat and wage upon
To build that amphitheatre and devise.

---

6. Explicit . . . tercia] "The second part ends here. The third part follows."

And to observe all rites and sacrifice,
Over the eastern gate, and high above,
For worship of Queen Venus, god of love,
He built an altar and an oratory;
And westward, being mindful of the glory
Of Mars, he straightway builded such another
As cost a deal of gold and many a bother.
And northward, in a turret on the wall,
Of alabaster white and red coral,
An oratory splendid as could be,
In honour of Diana's chastity,
Duke Thesëus wrought out in noble wise.
　　But yet have I forgot to advertise
The noble carvings and the portraitures,
The shapes, the countenances, the figures
That all were in these oratories three.
　　First, in the fane[7] of Venus, one might see,
Wrought on the wall, and piteous to behold,
The broken slumbers and the sighing cold,
The sacred tears and the lamenting dire,
The fiery throbbing of the strong desire,
That all love's servants in this life endure;
The vows that all their promises assure;
Pleasure and hope, desire, foolhardiness,
Beauty, youth, bawdiness, and riches, yes,
Charms, and all force, and lies, and flattery,
Expense, and labour; aye, and Jealousy
That wore of marigolds a great garland
And had a cuckoo sitting on her hand;
Carols and instruments and feasts and dances,
Lust and array, and all the circumstances
Of love that I may reckon or ever shall,
In order they were painted on the wall,
Aye, and more, too, than I have ever known.
For truly, all the Mount of Citheron,
Where Venus has her chief and favoured dwelling,
Was painted on that wall, beyond my telling,
With all the gardens in their loveliness.
Nor was forgot the gate-guard Idleness,

7. *fane*] temple, church.

Nor fair Narcissus of the years long gone,
Nor yet the folly of King Solomon,
No, nor the giant strength of Hercules,
Nor Circe's and Medea's sorceries,
Nor Turnus with his hardy, fierce courage,
Nor the rich Croesus, captive in his age.
Thus may be seen that wisdom, nor largess,
Beauty, nor skill, nor strength, nor hardiness,
May with Queen Venus share authority;
For as she wills, so must the whole world be.
Lo, all these folk were so caught in her snare
They cried aloud in sorrow and in care.
Here let suffice examples one or two,
Though I might give a thousand more to you.
    The form of Venus, glorious as could be,
Was naked, floating on the open sea,
And from the navel down all covered was
With green waves, bright as ever any glass.
A citole[8] in her small right hand had she,
And on her head, and beautiful to see,
A garland of red roses, sweet smelling;
Above her swirled her white doves, fluttering.
Before her stood her one son, Cupido,
Whose two white wings upon his shoulders grow;
And blind he was, as it is often seen;
A bow he bore, and arrows bright and keen.
    Why should I not as well, now, tell you all
The portraiture that was upon the wall
Within the fane of mighty Mars the red?
In length and breadth the whole wall was painted
Like the interior of that grisly place,
The mighty temple of great Mars in Thrace,
In that same cold and frosty region where
Mars to his supreme mansion may repair.
    First, on the wall was limned a vast forest
Wherein there dwelt no man nor any beast,
With knotted, gnarled, and leafless trees, so old
The sharpened stumps were dreadful to behold;
Through which there ran a rumbling, even now,

---

8. *citole*] a kind of small dulcimer.

As if a storm were breaking every bough;
And down a hill, beneath a sharp descent,
The temple stood of Mars armipotent,
Wrought all of burnished steel, whereof the gate
Was grim like death to see, and long, and strait.
And therefrom raged a wind that seemed to shake
The very ground, and made the great doors quake.
The northern light in at those same doors shone,
For window in that massive wall was none
Through which a man might any light discern.
The doors were all of adamant eterne,
Rivetted on both sides, and all along,
With toughest iron; and to make it strong,
Each pillar that sustained this temple grim
Was thick as tun, of iron bright and trim.
There saw I first the dark imagining
Of felony, and all the compassing;
And cruel anger, red as burning coal;
Pickpurses, and the dread that eats the soul;
The smiling villain, hiding knife in cloak;
The farm barns burning, and the thick black smoke;
The treachery of murder done in bed;
The open battle, with the wounds that bled;
Contest, with bloody knife and sharp menace;
And loud with creaking was that dismal place.
The slayer of himself, too, saw I there,
His very heart's blood matted in his hair;
The nail that's driven in the skull by night;
The cold plague-corpse, with gaping mouth upright.
In middle of the temple sat Mischance,
With gloomy, grimly woeful countenance.
And saw I Madness laughing in his rage;
Armed risings, and outcries, and fierce outrage;
The carrion in the bush, with throat wide carved;
A thousand slain, nor one by plague, nor starved.
The tyrant, with the spoils of violent theft;
The town destroyed, in ruins, nothing left.
And saw I burnt the ships that dance by phares;[9]
The hunter strangled by the fierce wild bears;

9. *phares*] a lighthouse (pharos), or a strait lighted by a pharos.

The sow chewing the child right in the cradle;
The cook well scalded, spite of his long ladle.
Nothing was lacking of Mars' evil part:
The carter over-driven by his cart,
Under a wheel he lay low in the dust.
There were likewise in Mars' house, as needs must,
The surgeon, and the butcher, and the smith
Who forges sharp swords and great ills therewith.
And over all, depicted in a tower,
Sat Conquest, high in honour and in power,
Yet with a sharp sword hanging o'er his head
But by the tenuous twisting of a thread.
Depicted was the death of Julius,
Of Nero great, and of Antonius;
And though at that same time they were unborn,
There were their deaths depicted to adorn
The menacing of Mars, in likeness sure;
Things were so shown, in all that portraiture,
As are fore-shown among the stars above,
Who shall be slain in war or dead for love.
Suffice one instance from old plenitude,
I could not tell them all, even if I would.
    Mars' image stood upon a chariot,
Armed, and so grim that mad he seemed, God wot;
And o'er his head two constellations shone
Of stars that have been named in writings known,
One being Puella, and one Rubeus.
This god of armies was companioned thus:
A wolf there was before him, at his feet,
Red-eyed, and of a dead man he did eat.
A cunning pencil there had limned this story
In reverence of Mars and of his glory.
    Now to the temple of Diana chaste,
As briefly as I can, I'll pass in haste,
To lay before you its description well.
In pictures, up and down, the wall could tell
Of hunting and of modest chastity.
There saw I how Callisto fared when she
(Diana being much aggrieved with her)
Was changed from woman into a she-bear,
And after, made into the lone Pole Star;

There was it; I can't tell how such things are.
Her son, too, is a star, as men may see.
There saw I Daphne turned into a tree
(I do not mean Diana, no, but she,
Penëus' daughter, who was called Daphne).
I saw Actaeon made a hart all rude
For punishment of seeing Diana nude;
I saw, too, how his fifty hounds had caught
And him were eating, since they knew him not.
And painted farther on, I saw before
How Atalanta hunted the wild boar;
And Meleager, and many another there,
For which Diana wrought him woe and care.
There saw I many another wondrous tale
From which I will not now draw memory's veil.
This goddess on an antlered hart was set,
With little hounds about her feet, and yet
Beneath her perfect feet there was a moon,
Waxing it was, but it should wane full soon.
In robes of yellowish green her statue was,
She'd bow in hand and arrows in a case.
Her eyes were downcast, looking at the ground,
Where Pluto in his dark realm may be found.
Before her was a woman travailing,
Who was so long in giving birth, poor thing,
That pitifully Lucina did she call,
Praying, "Oh help, for thou may'st best of all!"
Well could he paint, who had this picture wrought,
With many a florin he'd his colours bought.

    But now the lists were done, and Thesëus,
Who at so great cost had appointed thus
The temples and the circus, as I tell,
When all was done, he liked it wondrous well.
But hold I will from Thesëus, and on
To speak of Arcita and Palamon.
    The day of their return is forthcoming,
When each of them a hundred knights must bring
The combat to support, as I have told;
And into Athens, covenant to uphold,
Has each one ridden with his hundred knights,
Well armed for war, at all points, in their mights.

And certainly, 'twas thought by many a man
That never, since the day this world began,
Speaking of good knights hardy of their hands,
Wherever God created seas and lands,
Was, of so few, so noble company.
For every man that loved all chivalry,
And eager was to win surpassing fame,
Had prayed to play a part in that great game;
And all was well with him who chosen was.
For if there came tomorrow such a case,
You know right well that every lusty knight
Who loves the ladies fair and keeps his might,
Be it in England, aye or otherwhere,
Would wish of all things to be present there
To fight for some fair lady. *Ben'cite!*
'Twould be a pleasant goodly sight to see!
    And so it was with those with Palamon.
With him there rode of good knights many a one;
Some would be armoured in a habergeon
And in a breastplate, under light jupon;
And some wore breast- and back-plates thick and large;
And some would have a Prussian shield, or targe;
Some on their very legs were armoured well,
And carried axe, and some a mace of steel.
There is no new thing, now, that is not old.
And so they all were armed, as I have told,
To his own liking and design, each one.
    There might you see, riding with Palamon,
Lycurgus' self, the mighty king of Thrace;
Black was his beard and manly was his face.
The eyeballs in the sockets of his head,
They glowed between a yellow and a red.
And like a griffon glared he round about
From under bushy eyebrows thick and stout.
His limbs were large, his muscles hard and strong,
His shoulders broad, his arms both big and long,
And, as the fashion was in his country,
High in a chariot of gold stood he,
With four white bulls in traces, to progress.
Instead of coat-of-arms above harness,
With yellow claws preserved and bright as gold,

He wore a bear-skin, black and very old.
His long combed hair was hanging down his back,
As any raven's feather it was black:
A wreath of gold, arm-thick, of heavy weight,
Was on his head, and set with jewels great,
Of rubies fine and perfect diamonds.
About his car there circled huge white hounds,
Twenty or more, as large as any steer,
To hunt the lion or the antlered deer;
And so they followed him, with muzzles bound,
Wearing gold collars with smooth rings and round.
A hundred lords came riding in his rout,
All armed at point, with hearts both stern and stout.
    With Arcita, in tales men call to mind,
The great Emetrëus, a king of Ind,
Upon a bay steed harnessed all in steel,
Covered with cloth of gold, all diapered well,
Came riding like the god of arms, great Mars.
His coat-of-arms was cloth of the Tartars,
Begemmed with pearls, all white and round and great.
Of beaten gold his saddle, burnished late;
A mantle from his shoulders hung, the thing
Close-set with rubies red, like fire blazing.
His crisp hair all in bright ringlets was run,
Yellow as gold and gleaming as the sun.
His nose was high, his eyes a bright citrine,
His lips were full, his colouring sanguine,
And a few freckles on his face were seen,
None either black or yellow, but the mean;
And like a lion he his glances cast.
Not more than five-and-twenty years he'd past.
His beard was well beginning, now, to spring;
His voice was as a trumpet thundering.
Upon his brows he wore, of laurel green,
A garland, fresh and pleasing to be seen.
Upon his wrist he bore, for his delight,
An eagle tame, as any lily white.
A hundred lords came riding with him there,
All armed, except their heads, in all their gear,
And wealthily appointed in all things.
For, trust me well, that dukes and earls and kings

Were gathered in this noble company
For love and for increase of chivalry.
About this king there ran, on every side,
Many tame lions and leopards in their pride.
And in such wise these mighty lords, in sum,
Were, of a Sunday, to the city come
About the prime, and in the town did light.
    This Thesëus, this duke, this noble knight,
When he'd conducted them to his city,
And quartered them, according to degree,
He feasted them, and was at so much pains
To give them ease and honour, of his gains,
That men yet hold that never human wit,
Of high or low estate, could better it.
The minstrelsy, the service at the feast,
The great gifts to the highest and the least,
The furnishings of Thesëus' rich palace,
Who highest sat or lowest on the dais,
What ladies fairest were or best dandling,
Or which of them could dance the best, or sing,
Or who could speak most feelingly of love,
Or what hawks sat upon the perch above,
Or what great hounds were lying on the floor —
Of all these I will make no mention more;
But tell my tale, for that, I think, is best;
Now comes the point, and listen if you've zest.
    That Sunday night, ere day began to spring,
When Palamon the earliest lark heard sing,
Although it lacked two hours of being day,
Yet the lark sang, and Palamon sang a lay.
With pious heart and with a high courage
He rose, to go upon a pilgrimage
Unto the blessed Cytherea's shrine
(I mean Queen Venus, worthy and benign).
And at her hour he then walked forth apace
Out to the lists wherein her temple was,
And down he knelt in manner to revere,
And from a full heart spoke as you shall hear.
    "Fairest of fair, O lady mine, Venus,
Daughter of Jove and spouse to Vulcanus,
Thou gladdener of the Mount of Citheron,

By that great love thou borest to Adon,
Have pity on my bitter tears that smart
And hear my humble prayer within thy heart.
Alas! I have no words in which to tell
The effect of all the torments of my hell;
My heavy heart its evils can't bewray;
I'm so confused I can find naught to say.
But mercy, lady bright, that knowest well
My heart, and seëst all the ills I feel,
Consider and have ruth upon my sore
As truly as I shall, for evermore,
Well as I may, thy one true servant be,
And wage a war henceforth on chastity.
If thou wilt help, thus do I make my vow,
To boast of knightly skill I care not now,
Nor do I ask tomorrow's victory,
Nor any such renown, nor vain glory
Of prize of arms, blown before lord and churl,
But I would have possession of one girl,
Of Emily, and die in thy service;
Find thou the manner how, and in what wise.
For I care not, unless it better be,
Whether I vanquish them or they do me,
So I may have my lady in my arms.
For though Mars is the god of war's alarms,
Thy power is so great in Heaven above,
That, if it be thy will, I'll have my love.
In thy fane will I worship always, so
That on thine altar, where'er I ride or go,
I will lay sacrifice and thy fires feed.
And if thou wilt not so, O lady, cede,
I pray thee, that tomorrow, with a spear,
Arcita bear me through the heart, just here.
For I'll care naught, when I have lost my life,
That Arcita may win her for his wife.
This the effect and end of all my prayer,
Give me my love, thou blissful lady fair."
    Now when he'd finished all the orison,
His sacrifice he made, this Palamon,
Right piously, with all the circumstance,
Albeit I tell not now his observance.

But at the last the form of Venus shook
And gave a sign, and thereupon he took
This as acceptance of his prayer that day.
For though the augury showed some delay,
Yet he knew well that granted was his boon;
And with glad heart he got him home right soon.
    Three hours unequal[10] after Palamon
To Venus' temple at the lists had gone,
Up rose the sun and up rose Emily,
And to Diana's temple did she hie.
Her maidens led she thither, and with them
They carefully took fire and each emblem,
And incense, robes, and the remainder all
Of things for sacrifice ceremonial.
There was not one thing lacking; I'll but add
The horns of mead, as was a way they had.
In smoking temple, full of draperies fair,
This Emily with young heart debonnaire,
Her body washed in water from a well;
But how she did the rite I dare not tell,
Except it be at large, in general;
And yet it was a thing worth hearing all;
When one's well meaning, there is no transgression;
But it is best to speak at one's discretion.
Her bright hair was unbound, but combed withal;
She wore of green oak leaves a coronal
Upon her lovely head. Then she began
Two fires upon the altar stone to fan,
And did her ceremonies as we're told
In Statius' *Thebaid* and books as old.
When kindled was the fire, with sober face
Unto Diana spoke she in that place.
    "O thou chaste goddess of the wildwood green,
By whom all heaven and earth and sea are seen,
Queen of the realm of Pluto, dark and low,
Goddess of maidens, that my heart dost know
For all my years, and knowest what I desire,
Oh, save me from thy vengeance and thine ire

10. *hours unequal*] hours formed by dividing the daylight by twelve. Hence, in May, hours of longer duration than sixty minutes.

That on Actaeon fell so cruelly.
Chaste goddess, well indeed thou knowest that I
Desire to be a virgin all my life,
Nor ever wish to be man's love or wife.
I am, thou know'st, yet of thy company,
A maid, who loves the hunt and venery,
And to go rambling in the greenwood wild,
And not to be a wife and be with child.
I do not crave the company of man.
Now help me, lady, since thou may'st and can,
By the three beings who are one in thee.
For Palamon, who bears such love to me,
And for Arcita, loving me so sore,
This grace I pray thee, without one thing more,
To send down love and peace between those two,
And turn their hearts away from me: so do
That all their furious love and their desire,
And all their ceaseless torment and their fire
Be quenched or turned into another place;
And if it be thou wilt not show this grace,
Or if my destiny be moulded so
That I must needs have one of these same two,
Then send me him that most desires me.
Behold, O goddess of utter chastity,
The bitter tears that down my two cheeks fall.
Since thou art maid and keeper of us all,
My maidenhead keep thou, and still preserve,
And while I live a maid, thee will I serve."
  The fires blazed high upon the altar there,
While Emily was saying thus her prayer,
But suddenly she saw a sight most quaint,
For there, before her eyes, one fire went faint,
Then blazed again; and after that, anon,
The other fire was quenched, and so was gone.
And as it died it made a whistling sound,
As do wet branches burning on the ground,
And from the brands' ends there ran out, anon,
What looked like drops of blood, and many a one;
At which so much aghast was Emily
That she was near dazed, and began to cry,
For she knew naught of what it signified;

But only out of terror thus she cried
And wept, till it was pitiful to hear.
But thereupon Diana did appear,
With bow in hand, like any right huntress,
And said: "My daughter, leave this heaviness.
Among the high gods it has been affirmed,
And by eternal written word confirmed,
That you shall be the wife of one of those
Who bear for you so many cares and woes;
But unto which of them I may not tell.
I can no longer tarry, so farewell.
The fires that on my altar burn incense
Should tell you everything, ere you go hence,
Of what must come of love in this your case."
    And with that word the arrows of the chase
The goddess carried clattered and did ring,
And forth she went in mystic vanishing;
At which this Emily astonished was,
And said she then: "Ah, what means this, alas!
I put myself in thy protection here,
Diana, and at thy disposal dear."
    And home she wended, then, the nearest way.
This is the purport; there's no more to say.
    At the next hour of Mars, and following this,
Arcita to the temple walked, that is
Devoted to fierce Mars, to sacrifice
With all the ceremonies, pagan-wise.
With sobered heart and high devotion, on
This wise, right thus he said his orison.
    "O mighty god that in the regions cold
Of Thrace art honoured, where thy lordships hold,
And hast in every realm and every land
The reins of battle in thy guiding hand,
And givest fortune as thou dost devise,
Accept of me my pious sacrifice.
If so it be that my youth may deserve,
And that my strength be worthy found to serve
Thy godhead, and be numbered one of thine,
Then pray I thee for ruth on pain that's mine.
For that same pain and even that hot fire
Wherein thou once did'st burn with deep desire,

When thou did'st use the marvelous beauty
Of fair young wanton Venus, fresh and free,
And had'st her in thine arms and at thy will
(Howbeit with thee, once, all the chance fell ill,
And Vulcan caught thee in his net, whenas
He found thee lying with his wife, alas!) —
For that same sorrow that was in thy heart,
Have pity, now, upon my pains that smart.
I'm young, and little skilled, as knowest thou,
With love more hurt and much more broken now
Than ever living creature was, I'm sure;
For she who makes me all this woe endure,
Whether I float or sink cares not at all,
And ere she'll hear with mercy when I call,
I must by prowess win her in this place;
And well I know, too, without help and grace
Of thee, my human strength shall not avail.
Then help me, lord, tomorrow not to fail,
For sake of that same fire that once burned thee,
The which consuming fire so now burns me;
And grant, tomorrow, I have victory.
Mine be the toil, and thine the whole glory!
Thy sovereign temple will I honour most
Of any spot, and toil and count no cost
To pleasure thee and in thy craft have grace,
And in thy fane my banner will I place,
And all the weapons of my company;
And evermore, until the day I die,
Eternal fire shalt thou before thee find.
Moreover, to this vow myself I bind:
My beard, my hair that ripples down so long,
That never yet has felt the slightest wrong
Of razor or of shears, to thee I'll give,
And be thy loyal servant while I live.
Now, lord, have pity on my sorrows sore;
Give me the victory. I ask no more."
    With ended prayer of Arcita the young,
The rings that on the temple door were hung,
And even the doors themselves, rattled so fast
That this Arcita found himself aghast.
The fires blazed high upon the altar bright,

Until the entire temple shone with light;
And a sweet odour rose up from the ground;
And Arcita whirled then his arm around,
And yet more incense on the fire he cast,
And did still further rites; and at the last
The armour of God Mars began to ring,
And with that sound there came a murmuring,
Low and uncertain, saying: "Victory!"
For which he gave Mars honour and glory.
And thus in joy and hope, which all might dare,
Arcita to his lodging then did fare,
Fain[11] of the fight as fowl is of the sun.
　　But thereupon such quarrelling was begun,
From this same granting, in the heaven above,
'Twixt lovely Venus, goddess of all love,
And Mars, the iron god armipotent,
That Jove toiled hard to make a settlement;
Until the sallow Saturn, calm and cold,
Who had so many happenings known of old,
Found from his full experience the art
To satisfy each party and each part.
For true it is, age has great advantage;
Experience and wisdom come with age;
Men may the old out-run, but not out-wit.
Thus Saturn, though it scarcely did befit
His nature so to do, devised a plan
To quiet all the strife, and thus began:
　　"Now my dear daughter Venus," quoth Saturn,
"My course, which has so wide a way to turn,
Has power more than any man may know.
Mine is the drowning in the sea below;
Mine is the dungeon underneath the moat;
Mine is the hanging and strangling by the throat;
Rebellion, and the base crowd's murmuring,
The groaning and the private poisoning,
And vengeance and amercement — all are mine,
While yet I dwell within the Lion's sign.
Mine is the ruining of all high halls,
And tumbling down of towers and of walls

11. *Fain*] desirous.

Upon the miner and the carpenter.
I struck down Samson, that pillar shaker;
And mine are all the maladies so cold,
The treasons dark, the machinations old;
My glance is father of all pestilence.
Now weep no more. I'll see, with diligence,
That Palamon, who is your own true knight,
Shall have his lady, as you hold is right.
Though Mars may help his man, yet none the less
Between you two there must come sometime peace,
And though you be not of one temperament,
Causing each day such violent dissent,
I am your grandsire and obey your will;
Weep then no more, your pleasure I'll fulfill."
    Now will I cease to speak of gods above,
Of Mars and Venus, goddess of all love,
And tell you now, as plainly as I can,
The great result, for which I first began.

Explicit tercia pars.
Sequitur pars quarta.[12]

Great was the fête in Athens on that day,
And too, the merry season of the May
Gave everyone such joy and such pleasance
That all that Monday they'd but joust and dance,
Or spend the time in Venus' high service.
But for the reason that they must arise
Betimes, to see the heralded great fight,
All they retired to early rest that night.
And on the morrow, when that day did spring,
Of horse and harness, noise and clattering,
There was enough in hostelries about.
And to the palace rode full many a rout
Of lords, bestriding steeds and on palfreys.
There could you see adjusting of harness,
So curious and so rich, and wrought so well
Of goldsmiths' work, embroidery, and of steel;
The shields, the helmets bright, the gay trappings,

12. Explicit . . . quarta] "The third part ends here. The fourth part follows."

The gold-hewn casques, the coats-of-arms, the rings,
The lords in vestments rich, on their coursers,
Knights with their retinues and also squires;
The rivetting of spears, the helm-buckling,
The strapping of the shields, and thong-lacing—
In their great need, not one of them was idle;
The frothing steeds, champing the golden bridle,
And the quick smiths, and armourers also,
With file and hammer spurring to and fro;
Yeoman, and peasants with short staves were out,
Crowding as thick as they could move about;
Pipes, trumpets, kettledrums, and clarions,
That in the battle sound such grim summons;
The palace full of people, up and down,
Here three, there ten, debating the renown
And questioning about these Theban knights,
Some put it thus, some said, "It's so by rights."
Some held with him who had the great black beard,
Some with the bald-heads, some with the thick haired;
Some said, "He looks grim, and he'll fight like hate;
He has an axe of twenty pound in weight."
And thus the hall was full of gossiping
Long after the bright sun began to spring.
   The mighty Thesëus, from sleep awakened
By songs and all the noise that never slackened,
Kept yet the chamber of this rich palace,
Till the two Theban knights, with equal grace
And honour, were ushered in with flourish fitting.
Duke Thesëus was at a window sitting,
Arrayed as he were god upon a throne.
Then pressed the people thitherward full soon,
To see him and to do him reverence,
Aye, and to hear commands of sapience.
   A herald on a scaffold cried out "Ho!"
Till all the people's noise was stilled; and so,
When he observed that all were fallen still,
He then proclaimed the mighty ruler's will.
   "The duke our lord, full wise and full discreet,
Holds that it were but wanton waste to meet
And fight, these gentle folk, all in the guise
Of mortal battle in this enterprise.

Wherefore, in order that no man may die,
He does his earlier purpose modify.
No man, therefore, on pain of loss of life,
Shall any arrow, pole-axe, or short knife
Send into lists in any wise, or bring;
Nor any shortened sword, for point-thrusting,
Shall a man draw, or bear it by his side.
Nor shall a knight against opponent ride,
Save one full course, with any sharp-ground spear;
Unhorsed, a man may thrust with any gear.
And he that's overcome, should this occur,
Shall not be slain, but brought to barrier,
Whereof there shall be one on either side;
Let him be forced to go there and abide.
And if by chance the leader there must go,
Of either side, or slay his equal foe,
No longer, then, shall tourneying endure.
God speed you; go forth now, and lay on sure.
With long sword and with maces fight your fill.
Go now your ways; this is the lord duke's will."
  The voices of the people rent the skies,
Such was the uproar of their merry cries:
"Now God save such a lord, who is so good
He will not have destruction of men's blood!"
Up start the trumpets and make melody.
And to the lists rode forth the company,
In marshalled ranks, throughout the city large,
All hung with cloth of gold, and not with serge.
Full like a lord this noble duke did ride,
With the two Theban knights on either side;
And, following, rode the queen and Emily,
And, after, came another company
Of one and other, each in his degree.
And thus they went throughout the whole city,
And to the lists they came, all in good time.
The day was not yet fully come to prime
When throned was Theseus full rich and high,
And Queen Hippolyta and Emily,
While other ladies sat in tiers about.
Into the seats then pressed the lesser rout.
And westward, through the gate of Mars, right hearty,

Arcita and the hundred of his party
With banner red is entering anon;
And in that self-same moment, Palamon
Is under Venus, eastward in that place,
With banner white, and resolute of face.
In all the world, searching it up and down,
So equal were they all, from heel to crown,
There were no two such bands in any way.
For there was no man wise enough to say
How either had of other advantage
In high repute, or in estate, or age,
So even were they chosen, as I guess.
And in two goodly ranks they did then dress.
And when the name was called of every one,
That cheating in their number might be none,
Then were the gates closed, and the cry rang loud:
"Now do your devoir,[12] all you young knights proud!"
　　The heralds cease their spurring up and down;
Now ring the trumpets as the charge is blown;
And there's no more to say, for east and west
Two hundred spears are firmly laid in rest;
And the sharp spurs are thrust, now, into side.
Now see men who can joust and who can ride!
Now shivered are the shafts on bucklers thick;
One feels through very breast-bone the spear's prick;
Lances are flung full twenty feet in height;
Out flash the swords like silver burnished bright.
Helmets are hewed, the lacings ripped and shred;
Out bursts the blood, gushing in stern streams red.
With mighty maces bones are crushed in joust.
One through the thickest throng begins to thrust.
There strong steeds stumble now, and down goes all.
One rolls beneath their feet as rolls a ball.
One flails about with club, being overthrown,
Another, on a mailed horse, rides him down.
One through the body's hurt, and haled, for aid,
Spite of his struggles, to the barricade,
As compact was, and there he must abide;
Another's captured by the other side.

12. *devoir*] duty.

At times Duke Thesëus orders them to rest,
To eat a bite and drink what each likes best.
And many times that day those Thebans two
Met in the fight and wrought each other woe;
Unhorsed each has the other on that day.
No tigress in the vale of Galgophey,[13]
Whose little whelp is stolen in the light,
Is cruel to the hunter as Arcite
For jealousy is cruel to Palamon;
Nor in Belmarie, when the hunt is on
Is there a lion, wild for want of food,
That of his prey desires so much the blood
As Palamon the death of Arcite there.
Their jealous blows fall on their helmets fair;
Out leaps the blood and makes their two sides red.
    But sometime comes the end of every deed;
And ere the sun had sunk to rest in gold,
The mighty King Emetrëus did hold
This Palamon, as he fought with Arcite,
And made his sword deep in the flesh to bite;
And by the force of twenty men he's made,
Unyielded, to withdraw to barricade.
And, trying hard to rescue Palamon,
The mighty King Lycurgus is borne down;
And King Emetrëus, for all his strength,
Is hurled out of the saddle a sword's length,
So hits out Palamon once more, or ere
(But all for naught) he's brought to barrier.
His hardy heart may now avail him naught;
He must abide there now, being fairly caught
By force of arms, as by provision known.
    Who sorrows now but woeful Palamon,
Who may no more advance into the fight?
And when Duke Thesëus had seen this sight,
Unto the warriors fighting, every one,
He cried out: "Hold! No more! For it is done!
Now will I prove true judge, of no party.
Theban Arcita shall have Emily,
Who, by his fortune, has her fairly won."

13. *Galgophey*] probably the vale of Gargaphie, where Actæon was turned into a stag.

And now a noise of people is begun
For joy of this, so loud and shrill withal,
It seems as if the very lists will fall.
But now, what can fair Venus do above?
What says she now? What does this queen of love
But weep so fast, for thwarting of her will,
Her tears upon the lists begin to spill.
She said: "Now am I shamed and over-flung."
But Saturn said: "My daughter, hold your tongue.
Mars has his will, his knight has all his boon,
And, by my head, you shall be eased, and soon."
The trumpeters and other minstrelsy,
The heralds that did loudly yell and cry,
Were at their best for joy of Arcita.
But hear me further while I tell you — ah! —
The miracle that happened there anon.
This fierce Arcita doffs his helmet soon,
And mounted on a horse, to show his face,
He spurs from end to end of that great place,
Looking aloft to gaze on Emily;
And she cast down on him a friendly eye
(For women, generally speaking, go
Wherever Fortune may her favor show);
And she was fair to see, and held his heart.
But from the ground infernal furies start,
From Pluto sent, at instance of Saturn,
Whereat his horse, for fear, began to turn
And leap aside, all suddenly falling there;
And Arcita before he could beware
Was pitched upon the ground, upon his head,
And lay there, moving not, as he were dead,
His chest crushed in upon the saddle-bow.
And black he lay as ever coal, or crow,
So ran the surging blood into his face.
Anon they carried him from out that place,
With heavy hearts, to Thesëus' palace.
There was his harness cut away, each lace,
And swiftly was he laid upon a bed,
For he was yet alive and some words said,
Crying and calling after Emily.
Duke Thesëus, with all his company,

Is come again to Athens, his city,
With joyous heart and great festivity.
And though sore grieved for this unhappy fall,
He would not cast a blight upon them all.
Men said, too, that Arcita should not die,
But should be healed of all his injury.
And of another thing they were right fain,
Which was, that of them all no one was slain,
Though each was sore, and hurt, and specially one
Who'd got a lance-head thrust through his breast-bone.
For other bruises, wounds and broken arms,
Some of them carried salves and some had charms;
And medicines of many herbs, and sage
They drank, to keep their limbs from hemorrhage.
In all of which this duke, as he well can,
Now comforts and now honours every man,
And makes a revelry the livelong night
For all these foreign lords, as was but right.
Nor was there held any discomfiting,
Save from the jousts and from the tourneying.
For truly, there had been no cause for shame,
Since being thrown is fortune of the game;
Nor is it, to be led to barrier,
Unyielded, and by twenty knights' power,
One man alone, surrounded by the foe,
Driven by arms, and dragged out, heel and toe,
And with his courser driven forth with staves
Of men on foot, yeomen and serving knaves —
All this imputes to one no kind of vice,
And no man may bring charge of cowardice.
For which, anon, Duke Theseus bade cry,
To still all rancour and all keen envy,
The worth, as well of one side as the other,
As equal both, and each the other's brother;
And gave them gifts according to degree,
And held a three days' feast, right royally;
And then convoyed these kings upon their road
For one full day, and to them honour showed.
And home went every man on his right way.
There was naught more but "Farewell" and "Good-day."
I'll say no more of war, but turn upon

My tale of Arcita and Palamon.
　　Swells now Arcita's breast until the sore
Increases near his heart yet more and more.
The clotted blood, in spite of all leech-craft,
Rots in his bulk, and there is must be left,
Since no device of skillful blood-letting,
Nor drink of herbs, can help him in this thing.
The power expulsive, or virtue animal
Called from its use the virtue natural,
Could not the poison void, nor yet expel.
The tubes of both his lungs began to swell,
And every tissue in his breast, and down,
Is foul with poison and all rotten grown.
He gains in neither, in his strife to live,
By vomiting or taking laxative;
All is so broken in that part of him,
Nature retains no vigour there, nor vim.
And certainly, where Nature will not work,
It's farewell physic, bear the man to kirk![14]
The sum of all is, Arcita must die,
And so he sends a word to Emily,
And Palamon, who was his cousin dear;
And then he said to them as you shall hear.
　　"Naught may the woeful spirit in my heart
Declare one point of how my sorrows smart
To you, my lady, whom I love the most;
But I bequeath the service of my ghost
To you above all others, this being sure
Now that my life may here no more endure.
Alas, the woe! Alas, the pain so strong
That I for you have suffered, and so long!
Alas for death! Alas, my Emily!
Alas, the parting of our company!
Alas, my heart's own queen! Alas, my wife!
My soul's dear lady, ender of my life!
What is this world? What asks a man to have?
Now with his love, now in the cold dark grave
Alone, with never any company.
Farewell, my sweet foe! O my Emily!

14. *kirk*] church.

Oh, take me in your gentle arms, I pray,
For love of God, and hear what I will say.
    "I have here, with my cousin Palamon,
Had strife and rancour many a day that's gone,
For love of you and for my jealousy.
May Jove so surely guide my soul for me,
To speak about a lover properly,
With all the circumstances, faithfully —
That is to say, truth, honour, and knighthood,
Wisdom, humility and kinship good,
And generous soul and all the lover's art —
So now may Jove have in my soul his part
As in this world, right now, I know of none
So worthy to be loved as Palamon,
Who serves you and will do so all his life.
And if you ever should become a wife,
Forget not Palamon, the noble man."
    And with that word his speech to fail began,
For from his feet up to his breast had come
The cold of death, making his body numb.
And furthermore, from his two arms the strength
Was gone out, now, and he was lost, at length.
Only the intellect, and nothing more,
Which dwelt within his heart so sick and sore,
Began to fail now, when the heart felt death,
And his eyes darkened, and he failed of breath.
But on his lady turned he still his eye,
And his last word was, "Mercy, Emily!"
His spirit changed its house and went away.
As I was never there, I cannot say
Where; so I stop, not being a soothsayer;
Of souls here naught shall I enregister;
Nor do I wish their notions, now, to tell
Who write of them, though they say where they dwell.
Arcita's cold; Mars guides his soul on high;
Now will I speak forthwith of Emily.
    Shrieked Emily and howled now Palamon,
Till Theseüs his sister took, anon,
And bore her, swooning, from the corpse away.
How shall it help, to dwell the livelong day
In telling how she wept both night and morrow?

For in like cases women have such sorrow,
When their good husband from their side must go,
And, for the greater part, they take on so,
Or else they fall into such malady
That, at the last, and certainly, they die.
· Infinite were the sorrows and the tears ·
Of all old folk and folk of tender years
Throughout the town, at death of this Theban;
For him there wept the child and wept the man;
So great a weeping was not, 'tis certain,
When Hector was brought back, but newly slain,
To Troy. Alas, the sorrow that was there!
· Tearing of cheeks and rending out of hair.
"Oh why will you be dead," these women cry,
"Who had of gold enough, and Emily?"
No man might comfort then Duke Thesëus,
Excepting his old father, Ægëus,
Who knew this world's mutations, and men's own,
Since he had seen them changing up and down,
Joy after woe, and woe from happiness:
He showed them, by example, the process.
    "Just as there never died a man," quoth he,
"But he had lived on earth in some degree,
Just so there never lived a man," he said,
"In all this world, but must be sometime dead.
This world is but a thoroughfare of woe,
And we are pilgrims passing to and fro;
Death is the end of every worldly sore."
And after this, he told them yet much more
To that effect, all wisely to exhort
The people that they should find some comfort.
    Duke Thesëus now considered and with care
What place of burial he should prepare
For good Arcita, as it best might be,
And one most worthy of his high degree.
And at the last concluded, hereupon,
· That where at first Arcita and Palamon
Had fought for love, with no man else between,
There, in that very grove, so sweet and green,
Where he mused on his amorous desires
Complaining of love's hot and flaming fires,

He'd make a pyre and have the funeral
Accomplished there, and worthily in all.
And so he gave command to hack and hew
The ancient oaks, and lay them straight and true
In split lengths that would kindle well and burn.
His officers, with sure swift feet, they turn
And ride away to do his whole intent.
And after this Duke Thesëus straightway sent
For a great bier, and had it all o'er-spread
With cloth of gold, the richest that he had.
Arcita clad he, too, in cloth of gold;
White gloves were on his hands where they did fold;
Upon his head a crown of laurel green,
And near his hand a sword both bright and keen.
Then, having bared the dead face on the bier,
The duke so wept, 'twas pitiful to hear.
And, so that folk might see him, one and all,
When it was day he brought them to the hall,
Which echoed of their wailing cries anon.
    Then came this woeful Theban, Palamon,
With fluttery beard and matted, ash-strewn hair,
All in black clothes wet with his tears; and there,
Surpassing all in weeping, Emily,
The most affected of the company.
And so that every several rite should be
Noble and rich, and suiting his degree,
Duke Thesëus commanded that they bring
Three horses, mailed in steel all glittering,
And covered with Arcita's armour bright.
Upon these stallions, which were large and white,
There rode three men, whereof one bore the shield,
And one the spear he'd known so well to wield;
The third man bore his Turkish bow, nor less
Of burnished gold the quiver than harness;
And forth they slowly rode, with mournful cheer,
Toward that grove, as you shall further hear.
    The noblest Greeks did gladly volunteer
To bear upon their shoulders that great bier,
With measured pace and eyes gone red and wet,
Through all the city, by the wide main street,
Which was all spread with black, and, wondrous high,

Covered with this same cloth were houses nigh.
Upon the right hand went old Ægëus,
And on the other side Duke Thesëus,
With vessels in their hands, of gold right fine,
All filled with honey, milk, and blood, and wine;
And Palamon with a great company;
And after that came woeful Emily,
With fire in hands, as use was, to ignite
The sacrifice and set the pyre alight.
    Great labour and full great apparelling
Went to the service and the fire-making,
For to the skies that green pyre reached its top,
And twenty fathoms did the arms out-crop,
That is to say, the branches went so wide.
Full many a load of straw they did provide.
But how the fire was made to climb so high;
Or what names all the different trees went by,
As oak, fir, birch, asp, alder, poplar, holm,
Willow, plane, ash, box, chestnut, linden, elm,
Laurel, thorn, maple, beech, yew, dogwood tree,
Or how they were felled, sha'n't be told by me.
Nor how the wood-gods scampered up and down,
Driven from homes that they had called their own,
Wherein they'd lived so long at ease, in peace,
The nymphs, the fauns, the hamadryades;[15]
Nor how the beasts, for fear, and the birds, all
Fled, when that ancient wood began to fall;
Nor how aghast the ground was in the light,
Not being used to seeing the sun so bright;
Nor how the fire was started first with straw,
And then with dry wood, riven thrice by saw,
And then with green wood and with spicery,
And then with cloth of gold and jewellery,
And garlands hanging with full many a flower,
And myrrh, and incense, sweet as rose in bower;
Nor how Arcita lies among all this,
Nor what vast wealth about his body is;
Nor how this Emily, as was their way,
Lighted the sacred funeral fire, that day,

15. *hamadryades*] wood nymphs.

Nor how she swooned when men built up the fire,
Nor what she said, nor what was her desire;
No, nor what gems men on the fire then cast,
When the white flame went high and burned so fast;
Nor how one cast his shield, and one his spear,
And some their vestments, on that burning bier,
With cups of wine, and cups of milk, and blood,
Into that flame, which burned as wild-fire would;
Nor how the Greeks, in one huge wailing rout,
Rode slowly three times all the fire about,
Upon the left hand, with a loud shouting,
And three times more, with weapons clattering,
While thrice the women there raised up a cry;
Nor how was homeward led sad Emily;
Nor how Arcita burned to ashes cold;
Nor aught of how the lichwake they did hold
All that same night, nor how the Greeks did play
Who, naked, wrestled best, with oil anointed,
Nor who best bore himself in deeds appointed.
I will not even tell how they were gone
Home, into Athens, when the play was done;
But briefly to the point, now, will I wend
And make of this, my lengthy tale, an end.
    With passing in their length of certain years,
All put by was the mourning and the tears
Of Greeks, as by one general assent;
And then it seems there was a parliament
At Athens, upon certain points in case;
Among the which points spoken of there was
The ratifying of alliances
That should hold Thebes from all defiances.
Whereat this noble Thesëus, anon,
Invited there the gentle Palamon,
Not telling him what was the cause and why;
But in his mourning clothes, and sorrowfully,
He came upon that bidding, so say I.
And then Duke Thesëus sent for Emily.
When they were seated and was hushed the place,
And Thesëus had mused a little space,
Ere any word came from his full wise breast,
His two eyes fixed on whoso pleased him best,

Then with a sad face sighed he deep and still,
And after that began to speak his will.
   "The Primal Mover and the Cause above,
When first He forged the goodly chain of love,
Great the effect, and high was His intent;
Well knew He why, and what thereof He meant;
For with that goodly chain of love He bound
The fire, the air, the water, and dry ground
In certain bounds, the which they might not flee;
That same First Cause and Mover," then quoth he,
"Has stablished in this base world, up and down,
A certain length of days to call their own
For all that are engendered in this place,
Beyond the which not one day may they pace,
Though yet all may that certain time abridge;
Authority there needs none, I allege,
For it is well proved by experience,
Save that I please to clarify my sense.
Then may men by this order well discern
This Mover to be stable and eterne.
Well may man know, unless he be a fool,
That every part derives but from the whole.
For Nature has not taken his being
From any part and portion of a thing,
But from a substance perfect, stable aye,
And so continuing till changed away.
And therefore, of His Wisdom's Providence,
Has He so well established ordinance
That species of all things and all progressions,
If they'd endure, it must be by successions,
Not being themselves eternal, 'tis no lie:
This may you understand and see by eye.
   "Lo now, the oak, that has long nourishing
Even from the time that it begins to spring,
And has so long a life, as we may see,
Yet at the last all wasted is the tree.
   "Consider, too, how even the hard stone
Under our feet we tread each day upon
Yet wastes it, as it lies beside the way.
And the broad river will be dry some day.
And great towns wane; we see them vanishing.
Thus may we see the end to everything.

"Of man and woman just the same is true:
Needs must, in either season of the two,
That is to say, in youth or else in age,
All men perish, the king as well as page;
Some in their bed, and some in the deep sea,
And some in the wide field — as it may be;
There's naught will help; all go the same way. Aye,
Then may I say that everything must die.
Who causes this but Jupiter the King?
He is the Prince and Cause of everything,
Converting all back to that primal well
From which it was derived, 'tis sooth to tell.
And against this, for every thing alive,
Of any state, avails it not to strive.
    "Then is it wisdom, as it seems to me,
To make a virtue of necessity,
And calmly take what we may not eschew,
And specially that which to all is due.
Whoso would balk at aught, he does folly,
And thus rebels against His potency.
And certainly a man has most honour
In dying in his excellence and flower,
When he is certain of his high good name;
For then he gives to friend, and self, no shame.
And gladder ought a friend be of his death
When, in much honour, he yields up his breath,
Than when his name's grown feeble with old age;
For all forgotten, then, is his courage.
Hence it is best for all of noble name
To die when at the summit of their fame.
The contrary of this is wilfulness.
Why do we grumble? Why have heaviness
That good Arcita, chivalry's fair flower,
Is gone, with honour, in his best-lived hour.
Out of the filthy prison of this life?
Why grumble here his cousin and his wife
About his welfare, who loved them so well?
Can he thank them? Nay, God knows, not! Nor tell
How they his soul and their own selves offend,
Though yet they may not their desires amend.
    "What may I prove by this long argument
Save that we all turn to merriment,

After our grief, and give Jove thanks for grace.
And so, before we go from out this place,
I counsel that we make, of sorrows two,
One perfect joy, lasting for aye, for you;
And look you now, where most woe is herein,
There will we first amend it and begin.
    "Sister," quoth he, "you have my full consent,
With the advice of this my Parliament,
That gentle Palamon, your own true knight,
Who serves you well with will and heart and might,
And so has ever, since you knew him first —
That you shall, of your grace, allay his thirst
By taking him for husband and for lord:
Lend me your hand, for this is our accord.
Let now your woman's pity make him glad.
For he is a king's brother's son, by gad;
And though he were a poor knight bachelor,
Since he has served you for so many a year,
And borne for you so great adversity,
This ought to weigh with you, it seems to me,
For mercy ought to dominate mere right."
    Then said he thus to Palamon the knight:
"I think there needs but little sermoning
To make you give consent, now, to this thing.
Come near, and take your lady by the hand."
    Between them, then, was tied that nuptial band,
Which is called matrimony or marriage,
By all the council and the baronage.
And thus, in all bliss and with melody,
Has Palamon now wedded Emily.
And God, Who all this universe has wrought,
Send him His love, who has it dearly bought.
For now has Palamon, in all things, wealth,
Living in bliss, in riches, and in health;
And Emily loved him so tenderly,
And he served her so well and faithfully,
That never word once marred their happiness,
No jealousy, nor other such distress.
Thus ends now Palamon and Emily;
And may God save all this fair company! Amen.

HERE ENDS THE KNIGHT'S TALE

THE MILLER'S PROLOGUE

THE WORDS BETWEEN THE HOST
AND THE MILLER

NOW WHEN the knight had thus his story told,
In all the rout there was nor young nor old
But said it was a noble story, well
Worthy to be kept in mind to tell;
And specially the gentle folk, each one.
Our host, he laughed and swore, "So may I run,
But this goes well; unbuckled is the mail;[1]
Let's see now who can tell another tale:
For certainly the game is well begun.
Now shall you tell, sir monk, if't can be done,
Something with which to pay for the knight's tale."
   The miller, who with drinking was all pale,
So that unsteadily on his horse he sat,
He would not take off either hood or hat,
Nor wait for any man, in courtesy,
But all in Pilate's voice began to cry,
And by the Arms and Blood and Bones he swore,
"I have a noble story in my store,
With which I will requite the good knight's tale."
   Our host saw, then, that he was drunk with ale,
And said to him: "Wait, Robin, my dear brother,
Some better man shall tell us first another:
Submit and let us work on profitably."
   "Now by God's soul," cried he, "that will not I!
For I will speak, or else I'll go my way."
   Our host replied: "Tell on, then, till doomsday!
You are a fool, your wit is overcome."
   "Now hear me," said the miller, "all and some!
But first I make a protestation round
That I'm quite drunk, I know it by my sound:

1. *mail*] (male, in the original); a bag.

And therefore, if I slander or mis-say,
Blame it on ale of Southwark, so I pray;
For I will tell a legend and a life
Both of a carpenter and of his wife,
And how a scholar set[2] the good wright's cap."
   The reeve replied and said: "Oh, shut your trap,
Let be your ignorant drunken ribaldry!
It is a sin, and further, great folly
To asperse any man, or him defame,
And, too, to bring upon a man's wife shame.
There are enough of other things to say."
   This drunken miller spoke on in his way,
And said: "Oh, but my dear brother Oswald,
The man who has no wife is no cuckold.
But I say not, thereby, that you are one:
Many good wives there are, as women run,
And ever a thousand good to one that's bad,
As well you know yourself, unless you're mad.
Why are you angry with my story's cue?
I have a wife, begad, as well as you,
Yet I'd not, for the oxen of my plow,
Take on my shoulders more than is enow,
By judging of myself that I am one;
I will believe full well that I am none.
A husband must not be inquisitive
Of God, nor of his wife, while she's alive.
So long as he may find God's plenty there,
For all the rest he need not greatly care."
   What should I say, except this miller rare
He would forgo his talk for no man there,
But told his churlish tale in his own way:
I think I'll here re-tell it, if I may.
And therefore, every gentle soul, I pray
That for God's love you'll hold not what I say
Evilly meant, but that I must rehearse
All of their tales, the better and the worse,
Or else prove false to some of my design.
Therefore, who likes not this, let him, in fine,
Turn over page and choose another tale:

2. *set*] to set a cap, i.e., to befool, to make a cuckold of.

For he shall find enough, both great and small,
Of stories touching on gentility,
And holiness, and on morality;
And blame not me if you do choose amiss.
The miller was a churl, you well know this;
So was the reeve, and many another more,
And ribaldry they told from plenteous store.
Be then advised, and hold me free from blame;
Men should not be too serious at a game.

HERE ENDS THE PROLOGUE

THE MILLER'S TALE

O NCE ON A TIME was dwelling in Oxford
A wealthy lout who took in guests to board,
And of his craft he was a carpenter.
A poor scholar was lodging with him there,
Who'd learned the arts, but all his phantasy
Was turned to study of astrology;
And knew a certain set of theorems
And could find out by various stratagems,
If men but asked of him in certain hours
When they should have a drought or else have showers,
Or if men asked of him what should befall
To anything — I cannot reckon them all.
  This clerk was called the clever Nicholas;
Of secret loves he knew and their solace;
And he kept counsel, too, for he was sly
And meek as any maiden passing by.
He had a chamber in that hostelry,
And lived alone there, without company,
All garnished with sweet herbs of good repute;
And he himself sweet-smelling as the root
Of licorice, valerian, or setwall.
His *Almagest*, and books both great and small,
His astrolabe, belonging to his art,
His algorism stones[1] — all laid apart
On shelves that ranged beside his lone bed's head;
His press was covered with a cloth of red.
And over all there lay a psaltery
Whereon he made an evening's melody,
Playing so sweetly that the chamber rang;
And *Angelus ad virginem*[2] he sang;

---

1. *algorism stones*] counting stones.
2. Angelus ad virginem] "The Angel to the Virgin," a hymn on the Annunciation.

And after that he warbled the *King's Note*:[3]
Often in good voice was his merry throat.
And thus this gentle clerk his leisure spends
Supported by some income and his friends.
    This carpenter had lately wed a wife
Whom he loved better than he loved his life;
And she was come to eighteen years of age.
Jealous he was and held her close in cage.
For she was wild and young and he was old,
And deemed himself as like to be cuckold.
He knew not Cato, for his lore was rude:
That vulgar man should wed similitude.
A man should wed according to estate,
For youth and age are often in debate.
But now, since he had fallen in the snare,
He must endure, like other folk, his care.
    Fair was this youthful wife, and therewithal
As weasel's was her body slim and small.
A girdle wore she, barred and striped, of silk.
An apron, too, as white as morning milk
About her loins, and full of many a gore;
White was her smock, embroidered all before
And even behind, her collar round about,
Of coal-black silk, on both sides, in and out;
The strings of the white cap upon her head
Were, like her collar, black silk worked with thread;
Her fillet[4] was of wide silk worn full high:
And certainly she had a lickerish[5] eye.
She'd thinned out carefully her eyebrows two,
And they were arched and black as any sloe.
She was a far more pleasant thing to see
Than is the newly budded young pear-tree;
And softer than the wool is on a wether.[6]
Down from her girdle hung a purse of leather,
Tasselled with silk, with latten beading sown.
In all this world, searching it up and down,
So gay a little doll, I well believe,

3. King's Note] the name of a tune.
4. *fillet*] a strip of material, usually worn as a headband.
5. *lickerish*] greedy, desirous.
6. *wether*] a male sheep castrated before sexual maturity.

Or such a wench, there's no man can conceive.
Far brighter was the brilliance of her hue
Than in the Tower the gold coins minted new.
And songs came shrilling from her pretty head
As from a swallow's sitting on a shed.
Therewith she'd dance too, and could play and sham
Like any kid or calf about its dam.
Her mouth was sweet as bragget or as mead
Or hoard of apples laid in hay or weed.
Skittish she was as is a pretty colt,
Tall as a staff and straight as cross-bow bolt.
A brooch she wore upon her collar low,
As broad as boss of buckler did it show;
Her shoes laced up to where a girl's legs thicken.
She was a primrose, and a tender chicken
For any lord to lay upon his bed,
Or yet for any good yeoman to wed.
   Now, sir, and then, sir, so befell the case,
That on a day this clever Nicholas
Fell in with this young wife to toy and play,
The while her husband was down Osney way,
Clerks being as crafty as the best of us;
And unperceived he caught her by the puss,
Saying: "Indeed, unless I have my will,
For secret love of you, sweetheart, I'll spill."
And held her hard about the hips, and how! —
And said: "O darling, love me, love me now,
Or I shall die, and pray you God may save!"
   And she leaped as a colt does in the trave,[7]
And with her head she twisted fast away,
And said: "I will not kiss you, by my fay!
Why, let go," cried she, "let go, Nicholas!
Or I will call for help and cry 'alas!'
Do take your hands away, for courtesy!"
   This Nicholas for mercy then did cry,
And spoke so well, importuned her so fast
That she her love did grant him at the last,
And swore her oath, by Saint Thomas of Kent,
That she would be at his command, content,

---

7. *trave*] a frame for confining a horse or colt for shoeing.

As soon as opportunity she could spy.
    "My husband is so full of jealousy,
Unless you will await me secretly,
I know I'm just as good as dead," said she.
"You must keep all quite hidden in this case."
    "Nay, thereof worry not," said Nicholas,
"A clerk has lazily employed his while
If he cannot a carpenter beguile."
    And thus they were agreed, and then they swore
To wait a while, as I have said before.
When Nicholas had done thus every whit
And patted her about the loins a bit,
He kissed her sweetly, took his psaltery,
And played it fast and made a melody.
    Then fell it thus, that to the parish kirk,
The Lord Christ Jesus' own works for to work,
This good wife went, upon a holy day;
Her forehead shone as bright as does the May,
So well she'd washed it when she left off work.
    Now there was of that church a parish clerk
Whose name was (as folk called him) Absalom.
Curled was his hair, shining like gold, and from
His head spread fanwise in a thick bright mop;
'Twas parted straight and even on the top;
His cheek was red, his eyes grey as a goose;
With Saint Paul's windows cut upon his shoes,
He stood in red hose fitting famously.
And he was clothed full well and properly
All in a coat of blue, in which were let
Holes for the lacings, which were fairly set.
And over all he wore a fine surplice
As white as ever hawthorn spray, and nice.
A merry lad he was, so God me save,
And well could he let blood, cut hair, and shave,
And draw a deed or quitclaim, as might chance.
In twenty manners could he trip and dance,
After the school that reigned in Oxford, though,
And with his two legs swinging to and fro;
And he could play upon a violin;
Thereto he sang in treble voice and thin;
And as well could he play on his guitar.

In all the town no inn was, and no bar,
That he'd not visited to make good cheer,
Especially were lively barmaids there.
But, truth to tell, he was a bit squeamish
Of farting and of language haughtyish.
    This Absalom, who was so light and gay,
Went with a censer on the holy day,
Censing the wives like an enthusiast;
And on them many a loving look he cast,
Especially on this carpenter's goodwife.
To look at her he thought a merry life,
She was so pretty, sweet, and lickerous.
I dare well say, if she had been a mouse
And he a cat, he would have mauled her some.
    This parish clerk, this lively Absalom
Had in his heart, now, such a love-longing
That from no wife took he an offering;
For courtesy, he said, he would take none.
The moon, when it was night, full brightly shone,
And his guitar did Absalom then take,
For in love-watching he'd intent to wake.
And forth he went, jolly and amorous,
Until he came unto the carpenter's house
A little after cocks began to crow;
And took his stand beneath a shot-window[8]
That was let into the good wood-wright's wall.
He sang then, in his pleasant voice and small,
"Oh now, dear lady, if your will it be,
I pray that you will have some ruth on me,"
The words in harmony with his string-plucking.
This carpenter awoke and heard him sing,
And called unto his wife and said, in sum:
"What, Alison! Do you hear Absalom,
Who plays and sings beneath our bedroom wall?"
    And she said to her husband, therewithal:
"Yes, God knows, John, I hear it, truth to tell."
    So this went on; what is there better than well?
From day to day this pretty Absalom
So wooed her he was woebegone therefrom.

---

8. *shot-window*] a window opening (or containing a division that opens) on a hinge.

He lay awake all night and all the day;
He combed his spreading hair and dressed him gay;
By go-betweens and agents, too, wooed he,
And swore her loyal page he'd ever be.
He sang as tremulously as nightingale;
He sent her sweetened wine and well-spiced ale
And waffles piping hot out of the fire,
And, she being town-bred, mead for her desire.
For some are won by means of money spent,
And some by tricks, and some by long descent.
Once, to display his versatility,
He acted Herod on a scaffold high.
    But what availed it him in any case?
She was enamoured so of Nicholas
That Absalom might go and blow his horn;
He got naught for his labour but her scorn.
And thus she made of Absalom her ape,
And all his earnestness she made a jape.
For truth is in this proverb, and no lie,
Men say well thus: It's always he that's nigh
That makes the absent lover seem a sloth.
For now, though Absalom be wildly wroth,
Because he is so far out of her sight,
This handy Nicholas stands in his light.
    Now bear you well, you clever Nicholas!
For Absalom may wail and sing "Alas!"
And so it chanced that on a Saturday
This carpenter departed to Osney;
And clever Nicholas and Alison
Were well agreed to this effect: anon
This Nicholas should put in play a wile
The simple, jealous husband to beguile;
And if it chanced the game should go a-right,
She was to sleep within his arms all night,
For this was his desire, and hers also.
Presently then, and without more ado,
This Nicholas, no longer did he tarry,
But softly to his chamber did he carry
Both food and drink to last at least a day,
Saying that to her husband she should say—
If he should come to ask for Nicholas—

Why, she should say she knew not where he was,
For all day she'd not seen him, far or nigh;
She thought he must have got some malady,
Because in vain her maid would knock and call;
He'd answer not, whatever might befall.

And so it was that all that Saturday
This Nicholas quietly in chamber lay,
And ate and slept, or did what pleased him best,
Till Sunday when the sun had gone to rest.

This simple man with wonder heard the tale,
And marvelled what their Nicholas might ail,
And said: "I am afraid, by Saint Thomas,
That everything's not well with Nicholas.
God send he be not dead so suddenly!
This world is most unstable, certainly;
I saw, today, the corpse being borne to kirk
Of one who, but last Monday, was at work.
Go up," said he unto his boy anon,
"Call at his door, or knock there with a stone,
Learn how it is and boldly come tell me."

The servant went up, then, right sturdily,
And at the chamber door, the while he stood,
He cried and knocked as any madman would—
"What! How! What do you, Master Nicholay?
How can you sleep through all the livelong day?"

But all for naught, he never heard a word;
A hole he found, low down upon a board,
Through which the house cat had been wont to creep;
And to that hole he stooped, and through did peep,
And finally he ranged him in his sight.
This Nicholas sat gaping there, upright,
As if he'd looked too long at the new moon.
Downstairs he went and told his master soon
In what array he'd found this self-same man.

This carpenter to cross himself began,
And said: "Now help us, holy Frideswide!
Little a man can know what shall betide.
This man is fallen, with his astromy,[9]
Into some madness or some agony;

9. *astromy*] the carpenter's corrupted form of astronomy.

I always feared that somehow this would be!
Men should not meddle in God's privity.
Aye, blessed always be the ignorant man,
Whose creed is all he ever has to scan!
So fared another clerk with astromy;
He walked into the meadows for to pry
Into the stars, to learn what should befall,
Until into a clay-pit he did fall;
He saw not that. But yet, by Saint Thomas,
I'm sorry for this clever Nicholas.
He shall be scolded for his studying,
If not too late, by Jesus, Heaven's King!
 "Get me a staff, that I may pry before,
The while you, Robin, heave against the door.
We'll take him from this studying, I guess."
 And on the chamber door, then, he did press.
His servant was a stout lad, if a dunce,
And by the hasp he heaved it up at once;
Upon the floor that portal fell anon.
This Nicholas sat there as still as stone,
Gazing, with gaping mouth, straight up in air.
This carpenter thought he was in despair,
And took him by the shoulders, mightily,
And shook him hard, and cried out, vehemently:
"What! Nicholay! Why how now! Come, look down!
Awake, and think on Jesus' death and crown!
I cross you from all elves and magic wights!"
 And then the night-spell said he out, by rights,
At the four corners of the house about,
And at the threshold of the door, without: —
 "O Jesus Christ and good Saint Benedict,
Protect this house from all that may afflict,
For the night hag the white Paternoster! —
Where hast thou gone, Saint Peter's sister?"
And at the last this clever Nicholas
Began to sigh full sore, and said: "Alas!
Shall all the world be lost so soon again?"
 This carpenter replied: "What say you, then?
What! Think on God, as we do, men that swink."
 This Nicholas replied: "Go fetch me drink;
And afterward I'll tell you privately

A certain thing concerning you and me;
I'll tell it to no other man or men."

    This carpenter went down and came again,
And brought of potent ale a brimming quart;
And when each one of them had drunk his part,
Nicholas shut the door fast, and with that
He drew a seat and near the carpenter sat.

    He said: "Now, John, my good host, lief and dear,
You must upon your true faith swear, right here,
That to no man will you this word betray;
For it is Christ's own word that I will say,
And if you tell a man, you're ruined quite;
This punishment shall come to you, of right,
That if you're traitor you'll go mad—and should!"

    "Nay, Christ forbid it, for His holy blood!"
Said then this simple man: "I am no blab,
Nor, though I say it, am I fond of gab.
Say what you will, I never will it tell
To child or wife, by Him that harried Hell!"

    "Now, John," said Nicholas, "I will not lie;
But I've found out, from my astrology,
As I have looked upon the moon so bright,
That now, come Monday next, at nine of night,
Shall fall a rain so wildly mad as would
Have been, by half, greater than Noah's flood.
This world," he said, "in less time than an hour,
Shall all be drowned, so terrible is this shower;
Thus shall all mankind drown and lose all life."

    This carpenter replied: "Alas, my wife!
And shall she drown? Alas, my Alison!"
For grief of this he almost fell. Anon
He said: "Is there no remedy in this case?"

    "Why yes, good luck," said clever Nicholas,
"If you will work by counsel of the wise;
You must not act on what your wits advise.
For so says Solomon, and it's all true,
'Work by advice and thou shalt never rue.'
And if you'll act as counselled and not fail,
I undertake, without a mast or sail,
To save us all, aye you and her and me.
Haven't you heard of Noah, how saved was he,

Because Our Lord had warned him how to keep
Out of the flood that covered earth so deep?"
   "Yes," said this carpenter, "long years ago."
   "Have you not heard," asked Nicholas, "also
The sorrows of Noah and his fellowship
In getting his wife to go aboard the ship?
He would have rather, I dare undertake,
At that time, and for all the weather black,
That she had one ship for herself alone.
Therefore, do you know what would best be done?
This thing needs haste, and of a hasty thing
Men must not preach nor do long tarrying.
   "Presently go, and fetch here to this inn
A kneading-tub, or brewing vat, and win
One each for us, but see that they are large,
Wherein we may swim out as in a barge,
And have therein sufficient food and drink
For one day only; that's enough, I think.
The water will dry up and flow away
About the prime of the succeeding day.
But Robin must not know of this, your knave,
And even Jill, your maid, I may not save;
Ask me not why, for though you do ask me,
I will not tell you of God's privity.
Suffice you, then, unless your wits are mad,
To have as great a grace as Noah had.
Your wife I shall not lose, there is no doubt,
Go, now, your way, and speedily get about,
But when you have, for you and her and me,
Procured these kneading-tubs, or beer-vats, three,
Then you shall hang them near the roof-tree high,
That no man our purveyance may espy.
And when you thus have done, as I have said,
And have put in our drink and meat and bread,
Also an axe to cut the ropes in two
When the flood comes, that we may float and go,
And cut a hole, high up, upon the gable,
Upon the garden side, over the stable,
That we may freely pass forth on our way
When the great rain and flood are gone that day —
Then shall you float as merrily, I'll stake,

As does the white duck after the white drake.
Then I will call, 'Ho, Alison! Ho; John!
Be cheery, for the flood will pass anon.'
And you will say, 'Hail, Master Nicholay!
Good morrow, I see you well, for it is day!'
And then shall we be barons all our life
Of all the world, like Noah and his wife.

  "But of one thing I warn you now, outright.
Be well advised, that on that very night
When we have reached our ships and got aboard,
Not one of us must speak or whisper word,
Nor call, nor cry, but sit in silent prayer;
For this is God's own bidding, hence — don't dare!

  "Your wife and you must hang apart, that in
The night shall come no chance for you to sin
Either in looking or in carnal deed.
These orders I have told you, go, God speed!
Tomorrow night, when all men are asleep,
Into our kneading-tubs will we three creep
And sit there, still, awaiting God's high grace.
Go, now, your way, I have no longer space
Of time to make a longer sermoning.
Men say thus: 'Send the wise and say no thing.'
You are so wise it needs not that I teach;
Go, save our lives, and that I do beseech."

  This silly carpenter went on his way.
Often he cried "Alas!" and "Welaway!"
And to his wife he told all, privately;
But she was better taught thereof than he
How all this rigmarole was to apply.
Nevertheless she acted as she'd die,
And said: "Alas! Go on your way anon,
Help us escape, or we are lost, each one;
I am your true and lawfully wedded wife;
Go, my dear spouse, and help to save our life."

  Lo, what a great thing is affection found!
Men die of imagination, I'll be bound,
So deep an imprint may the spirit take.
This hapless carpenter began to quake;
He thought now, verily, that he could see
Old Noah's flood come wallowing like the sea

To drown his Alison, his honey dear.
He wept, he wailed, he made but sorry cheer,
He sighed and made full many a sob and sough.
He went and got himself a kneading-trough
And, after that, two tubs he somewhere found
And to his dwelling privately sent round,
And hung them near the roof, all secretly.
With his own hand, then, made he ladders three,
To climb up by the rungs thereof, it seems,
And reach the tubs left hanging to the beams;
And those he victualled, tubs and kneading-trough,
With bread and cheese and good jugged ale, enough
To satisfy the needs of one full day.
But ere he'd put all this in such array,
He sent his servants, boy and maid, right down
Upon some errand into London town.
And on the Monday, when it came on night,
He shut his door, without a candle-light,
And ordered everything as it should be.
And shortly after up they climbed, all three;
They sat while one might plow a furlong-way.
    "Now, by Our Father, hush!" said Nicholay,
And "Hush!" said John, and "Hush!" said Alison.
    This carpenter, his loud devotions done,
Sat silent, saying mentally a prayer,
And waiting for the rain, to hear it there.
    The deathlike sleep of utter weariness
Fell on this wood-wright even (as I guess)
About the curfew time, or little more;
For travail of his spirit he groaned sore,
And soon he snored, for badly his head lay.
Down by the ladder crept this Nicholay,
And Alison, right softly down she sped.
Without more words they went and got in bed
Even where the carpenter was wont to lie.
There was the revel and the melody!
And thus lie Alison and Nicholas,
In joy that goes by many an alias,
Until the bells for lauds began to ring
And friars to the chancel went to sing.
    This parish clerk, this amorous Absalom,

Whom love has made so woebegone and dumb,
Upon the Monday was down Osney way,
With company, to find some sport and play;
And there he chanced to ask a cloisterer,
Privately, after John the carpenter.
This monk drew him apart, out of the kirk,
And said: "I have not seen him here at work
Since Saturday; I think well that he went
For timber, that the abbot has him sent;
For he is wont for timber thus to go,
Remaining at the grange a day or so;
Or else he's surely at his house today;
But which it is I cannot truly say."

This Absalom right happy was and light,
And thought: "Now is the time to wake all night;
For certainly I saw him not stirring
About his door since day began to spring.
So may I thrive, as I shall, at cock's crow,
Knock cautiously upon that window low
Which is so placed upon his bedroom wall.
To Alison then will I tell of all
My love-longing, and thus I shall not miss
That at the least I'll have her lips to kiss.
Some sort of comfort shall I have, I say,
My mouth's been itching all this livelong day;
That is a sign of kissing at the least.
All night I dreamed, too, I was at a feast.
Therefore I'll go and sleep two hours away,
And all this night then will I wake and play."

And so when time of first cock-crow was come,
Up rose this merry lover, Absalom,
And dressed him gay and all at point-device,
But first he chewed some licorice and spice
So he'd smell sweet, ere he had combed his hair.
Under his tongue some bits of true-love[10] rare,
For thereby thought he to be more gracious.
He went, then, to the carpenter's dark house.
And silent stood beneath the shot-window;
Unto his breast it reached, it was so low;
And he coughed softly, in a low half tone:

---

10. *true-love*] probably herb paris.

"What do you, honeycomb, sweet Alison?
My cinnamon, my fair bird, my sweetie,
Awake, O darling mine, and speak to me!
It's little thought you give me and my woe,
Who for your love do sweat where'er I go.
Yet it's no wonder that I faint and sweat;
I long as does the lamb for mother's teat.
Truly, sweetheart, I have such love-longing
That like a turtle-dove's my true yearning;
And I can eat no more than can a maid."

   "Go from the window, jack-a-napes," she said,
"For, s'help me God, it is not 'come kiss me.'
I love another, or to blame I'd be,
Better than you, by Jesus, Absalom!
Go on your way, or I'll stone you therefrom,
And let me sleep, the fiends take you away!"

   "Alas," quoth Absalom, "and welaway!
That true love ever was so ill beset!
But kiss me, since you'll do no more, my pet,
For Jesus' love and for the love of me."

   "And will you go, then, on your way?" asked she.

   "Yes truly, darling," said this Absalom.

   "Then make you ready," said she, "and I'll come!"

   And unto Nicholas said she, low and still:
"Be silent now, and you shall laugh your fill."

   This Absalom plumped down upon his knees,
And said: "I am a lord in all degrees;
For after this there may be better still!
Darling, my sweetest bird, I wait your will."

   The window she unbarred, and that in haste.
"Have done," said she, "come on, and do it fast,
Before we're seen by any neighbour's eye."

   This Absalom did wipe his mouth all dry;
Dark was the night as pitch, aye dark as coal,
And through the window she put out her hole.
And Absalom no better felt nor worse,
But with his mouth he kissed her naked arse
Right greedily, before he knew of this.

   Aback he leapt—it seemed somehow amiss,
For well he knew a woman has no beard;
He'd felt a thing all rough and longish haired,
And said, "Oh fie, alas! What did I do?"

"Teehee!" she laughed, and clapped the window to;
And Absalom went forth a sorry pace.
    "A beard! A beard!" cried clever Nicholas,
"Now by God's *corpus*, this goes fair and well!"
    This hapless Absalom, he heard that yell,
And on his lip, for anger, he did bite;
And to himself he said, "I will requite!"
    Who vigorously rubbed and scrubbed his lips
With dust, with sand, with straw, with cloth, with chips,
But Absalom, and often cried "Alas!
My soul I give now unto Sathanas,
For rather far than own this town," said he,
"For this despite, it's well revenged I'd be.
Alas," said he, "from her I never blenched!"
    His hot love was grown cold, aye and all quenched;
For, from the moment that he'd kissed her arse,
For paramours he didn't care a curse,
For he was healed of all his malady;
Indeed all paramours he did defy,
And wept as does a child that has been beat.
With silent step he went across the street
Unto a smith whom men called Dan Jarvis,
Who in his smithy forged plow parts, that is
He sharpened shares and coulters busily.
This Absalom he knocked all easily,
And said, "Unbar here, Jarvis, for I come."
    "What! Who are you?"
                                    "It's I, it's Absalom."
    "What! Absalom! For Jesus Christ's sweet tree,
Why are you up so early? *Ben'cite!*
What ails you now, man? Some gay girl, God knows,
Has brought you on the jump to my bellows;
By Saint Neot, you know well what I mean."
    This Absalom cared not a single bean
For all this play, nor one word back he gave;
He'd more tow on his distaff, had this knave,
Than Jarvis knew, and said he: "Friend so dear,
This red-hot coulter in the fireplace here,
Lend it to me, I have a need for it,
And I'll return it after just a bit."
    Jarvis replied: "Certainly, were it gold

Or a purse filled with yellow coins untold,
Yet should you have it, as I am true smith;
But eh, Christ's foe! What will you do therewith?"
  "Let that," said Absalom, "be as it may;
I'll tell you all tomorrow, when it's day" —
And caught the coulter then by the cold steel
And softly from the smithy door did steal
And went again up to the wood-wright's wall.
He coughed at first, and then he knocked withal
Upon the window, as before, with care.
  This Alison replied: "Now who is there?
And who knocks so? I'll warrant it's a thief."
  "Why no," quoth he, "God knows, my sweet rose-leaf,
I am your Absalom, my own darling!
Of gold," quoth he, "I have brought you a ring;
My mother gave it me, as I'll be saved;
Fine gold it is, and it is well engraved;
This will I give you for another kiss."
  This Nicholas had risen for a piss,
And thought that it would carry on the jape
To have his arse kissed by this jack-a-nape.
And so he opened window hastily,
And put his arse out thereat, quietly,
Over the buttocks, showing the whole bum;
And thereto said this clerk, this Absalom,
"O speak, sweet bird, I know not where thou art."
This Nicholas just then let fly a fart
As loud as it had been a thunder-clap,
And well-nigh blinded Absalom, poor chap;
But he was ready with his iron hot
And Nicholas right in the arse he got.
  Off went the skin a hand's-breadth broad, about,
The coulter burned his bottom so, throughout,
That for the pain he thought that he should die.
And like one mad he started in to cry,
"Help! Water! Water! Help! For God's dear heart!"
  This carpenter out of his sleep did start,
Hearing that "Water!" cried as madman would,
And thought, "Alas, now comes down Noel's[11] flood!"

---

11. *Noel's*] the carpenter's corruption of "Noah's."

He struggled up without another word
And with his axe he cut in two the cord,
And down went all; he did not stop to trade
In bread or ale till he'd the journey made,
And there upon the floor he swooning lay.
   Up started Alison and Nicholay
And shouted "Help!" and "Hello!" down the street.
The neighbours, great and small, with hastening feet
Swarmed in the house to stare upon this man,
Who lay yet swooning, and all pale and wan;
For in the falling he had smashed his arm.
He had to suffer, too, another harm,
For when he spoke he was at once borne down
By clever Nicholas and Alison.
For they told everyone that he was odd;
He was so much afraid of "Noel's" flood,
Through fantasy, that out of vanity
He'd gone and bought these kneading-tubs, all three,
And that he'd hung them near the roof above;
And that he had prayed them, for God's dear love,
To sit with him and bear him company.
   The people laughed at all this fantasy;
Up to the roof they looked, and there did gape,
And so turned all his injury to a jape.
For when this carpenter got in a word,
'Twas all in vain, no man his reasons heard;
With oaths impressive he was so sworn down
That he was held for mad by all the town;
For every clerk did side with every other.
They said: "The man is crazy, my dear brother."
And everyone did laugh at all this strife.
   Thus futtered[12] was the carpenter's goodwife,
For all his watching and his jealousy;
And Absalom has kissed her nether eye;
And Nicholas is branded on the butt.
This tale is done, and God save all the rout!

HERE ENDS THE MILLER'S TALE

---

12. *futtered*] slept with.

THE WIFE OF BATH'S PROLOGUE

E XPERIENCE, though no authority
Were in this world, were good enough for me,
To speak of woe that is in all marriage;
For, masters, since I was twelve years of age,
Thanks be to God Who is for aye alive,
Of husbands at church door have I had five;
For men so many times have wedded me;
And all were worthy men in their degree.
But someone told me not so long ago
That since Our Lord, save once, would never go
To wedding (that at Cana in Galilee),
Thus, by this same example, showed He me
I never should have married more than once.
Lo and behold! What sharp words, for the nonce,
Beside a well Lord Jesus, God and man,
Spoke in reproving the Samaritan:
'For thou hast had five husbands,' thus said He,
'And he whom thou hast now to be with thee
Is not thine husband.' Thus He said that day,
But what He meant thereby I cannot say;
And I would ask now why that same fifth man
Was not husband to the Samaritan?
How many might she have, then, in marriage?
For I have never heard, in all my age,
Clear exposition of this number shown,
Though men may guess and argue up and down.
But well I know and say, and do not lie,
God bade us to increase and multiply;
That worthy text can I well understand.
And well I know He said, too, my husband
Should father leave, and mother, and cleave to me;
But no specific number mentioned He,
Whether of bigamy or octogamy;
Why should men speak of it reproachfully?
   Lo, there's the wise old king Dan Solomon;

103

I understand he had more wives than one;
And now would God it were permitted me
To be refreshed one half as oft as he!
Which gift of God he had for all his wives!
No man has such that in this world now lives.
God knows, this noble king, it strikes my wit,
The first night he had many a merry fit
With each of them, so much he was alive!
Praise be to God that I have wedded five!

> Of whom I did pick out and choose the best
> Both for their nether purse and for their chest.
> 1 Different schools make divers perfect clerks,
> Different methods learned in sundry works
> Make the good workman perfect, certainly.
> Of full five husbands tutoring am I.

Welcome the sixth whenever come he shall.
Forsooth, I'll not keep chaste for good and all;
When my good husband from the world is gone,
Some Christian man shall marry me anon;
For then, the apostle says that I am free
To wed, in God's name, where it pleases me.
He says that to be wedded is no sin;
Better to marry than to burn within.
What care I though folk speak reproachfully
Of wicked Lamech and his bigamy?
I know well Abraham was holy man,
And Jacob, too, as far as know I can;
And each of them had spouses more than two;
And many another holy man also.
Or can you say that you have ever heard
That God has ever by His express word
Marriage forbidden? Pray you, now, tell me;
Or where commanded He virginity?
I read as well as you no doubt have read
The apostle when he speaks of maidenhead;
He said, commandment of the Lord he'd none.
Men may advise a woman to be one,
But such advice is not commandment, no;
He left the thing to our own judgment so.

1. *Of whom . . . am I]* genuine lines carried in some manuscripts.

For had Lord God commanded maidenhood,
He'd have condemned all marriage as not good;
And certainly, if there were no seed sown,
Virginity — where then should it be grown?
Paul dared not to forbid us, at the least,
A thing whereof his Master'd no behest.
The dart is set up for virginity;
Catch it who can; who runs best let us see.
    "But this word is not meant for every wight,
But where God wills to give it, of His might.
I know well that the apostle was a maid;
Nevertheless, and though he wrote and said
He would that everyone were such as he,
All is not counsel to virginity;
And so to be a wife he gave me leave
Out of permission; there's no shame should grieve
In marrying me, if that my mate should die,
Without exception, too, of bigamy.
And though 'twere good no woman's flesh to touch,
He meant, in his own bed or on his couch;
For peril 'tis fire and tow to assemble;
You know what this example may resemble.
This is the sum: he held virginity
Nearer perfection than marriage for frailty.
And frailty's all, I say, save he and she
Would lead their lives throughout in chastity.
    "I grant this well, I have no great envy
Though maidenhood's preferred to bigamy;
Let those who will be clean, body and ghost,
Of my condition I will make no boast.
For well you know, a lord in his household,
He has not every vessel all of gold;
Some are of wood and serve well all their days.
God calls folk unto Him in sundry ways,
And each one has from God a proper gift,
Some this, some that, as pleases Him to shift.
    "Virginity is great perfection known,
And continence e'en with devotion shown.
But Christ, Who of perfection is the well,
Bade not each separate man he should go sell
All that he had and give it to the poor

And follow Him in such wise going before.
He spoke to those that would live perfectly;
And, masters, by your leave, such am not I.
I will devote the flower of all my age
To all the acts and harvests of marriage.
  "Tell me also, to what purpose or end
The genitals were made, that I defend,
And for what benefit was man first wrought?
Trust you right well, they were not made for naught.
Explain who will and argue up and down
That they were made for passing out, as known,
Of urine, and our two belongings small
Were just to tell a female from a male,
And for no other cause — ah, say you no?
Experience knows well it is not so;
And, so the clerics be not with me wroth,
I say now that they have been made for both,
That is to say, for duty and for ease
  In getting, when we do not God displease.
Why should men otherwise in their books set
That man shall pay unto his wife his debt?
Now wherewith should he ever make payment,
Except he used his blessed instrument?
Then on a creature were devised these things
For urination and engenderings.
  "But I say not that every one is bound,
Who's fitted out and furnished as I've found,
To go and use it to beget an heir;
Then men would have for chastity no care.
Christ was a maid, and yet shaped like a man,
And many a saint, since this old world began,
Yet has lived ever in perfect chastity.
I bear no malice to virginity;
Let such be bread of purest white wheat-seed,
And let us wives be called but barley bread;
And yet with barley bread (if Mark you scan)
Jesus Our Lord refreshed full many a man.
In such condition as God places us
I'll persevere, I'm not fastidious.
In wifehood I will use my instrument
As freely as my Maker has it sent.
If I be niggardly, God give me sorrow!

My husband he shall have it, eve and morrow,
When he's pleased to come forth and pay his debt.
I'll not delay, a husband I will get
Who shall be both my debtor and my thrall
And have his tribulations therewithal
Upon his flesh, the while I am his wife.
I have the power during all my life
Over his own good body, and not he.
For thus the apostle told it unto me;
And bade our husbands that they love us well.
And all this pleases me whereof I tell."
    Up rose the pardoner, and that anon.
"Now dame," said he, "by God and by Saint John,
You are a noble preacher in this case!
I was about to wed a wife, alas!
Why should I buy this on my flesh so dear?
No, I would rather wed no wife this year."
    "But wait," said she, "my tale is not begun;
Nay, you shall drink from out another tun
Before I cease, and savour worse than ale.
And when I shall have told you all my tale
Of tribulation that is in marriage,
Whereof I've been an expert all my age,
That is to say, myself have been the whip,
Then may you choose whether you will go sip
Out of that very tun which I shall broach.
Beware of it ere you too near approach;
For I shall give examples more than ten.
Whoso will not be warned by other men
By him shall other men corrected be.
The self-same words has written Ptolemy;
Read in his Almagest and find it there."
    "Lady, I pray you, if your will it were,"
Spoke up this pardoner, "as you began,
Tell forth your tale, nor spare for any man,
And teach us younger men of your technique."
    "Gladly," said she, "since it may please, not pique.
But yet I pray of all this company
That if I speak from my own phantasy,
They will not take amiss the things I say;
For my intention's only but to play.
    "Now, sirs, now will I tell you forth my tale.

And as I may drink ever wine and ale,
I will tell truth of husbands that I've had,
For three of them were good and two were bad.
The three were good men and were rich and old;
Not easily could they the promise hold
Whereby they had been bound to cherish me.
You know well what I mean by that, pardie!
So help me God, I laugh now when I think
How pitifully by night I made them swink;
And by my faith I set by it no store.
They'd given me their gold, and treasure more;
I needed not do longer diligence
To win their love, or show them reverence.
They all loved me so well, by God above,
I never did set value on their love!
A woman wise will strive continually
To get herself loved, when she's not, you see.
But since I had them wholly in my hand,
And since to me they'd given all their land,
Why should I take heed, then, that I should please,
Save it were for my profit or my ease?
I set them so to work, that, by my fay,
Full many a night they sighed out 'Welaway!'
The bacon was not brought them home, I trow,
That some men have in Essex at Dunmowe.
I governed them so well, by my own law,
That each of them was happy as a daw,
And fain to bring me fine things from the fair.
And they were right glad when I spoke them fair;
For God knows that I nagged them mercilessly.
     "Now hearken how I bore me properly,
All you wise wives that well can understand.
     "Thus shall you speak and wrongfully demand;
For half so brazenfacedly can no man
Swear to his lying as a woman can.
I say not this to wives who may be wise,
Except when they themselves do misadvise.
A wise wife, if she knows what's for her good,
Will swear the crow is mad, and in this mood
Call up for witness to it her own maid;
But hear me now, for this is what I said.

" 'Sir Dotard, is it thus you stand today?
Why is my neighbour's wife so fine and gay?
She's honoured over all where'er she goes;
I sit at home, I have no decent clo'es.
What do you do there at my neighbour's house?
Is she so fair? Are you so amorous?
Why whisper to our maid? *Benedicite!*
Sir Lecher old, let your seductions be!
And if I have a gossip or a friend,
Innocently, you blame me like a fiend
If I but walk, for company, to his house!
You come home here as drunken as a mouse,
And preach there on your bench, a curse on you!
You tell me it's a great misfortune, too,
To wed a girl who costs more than she's worth;
And if she's rich and of a higher birth,
You say it's torment to abide her folly
And put up with her pride and melancholy.
And if she be right fair, you utter knave,
You say that every lecher will her have;
She may no while in chastity abide
That is assailed by all and on each side.
    " 'You say, some men desire us for our gold,
Some for our shape and some for fairness told;
And some, that she can either sing or dance,
And some, for courtesy and dalliance;
Some for her hands and for her arms so small;
Thus all goes to the devil in your tale.
You say men cannot keep a castle wall
That's long assailed on all sides, and by all.
    " 'And if that she be foul, you say that she
Hankers for every man that she may see;
For like a spaniel will she leap on him
Until she finds a man to be victim;
And not a grey goose swims there in the lake
But finds a gander willing her to take.
You say, it is a hard thing to enfold
Her whom no man will in his own arms hold.
This say you, worthless, when you go to bed;
And that no wise man needs thus to be wed,
No, nor a man that hearkens unto Heaven.

With furious thunder-claps and fiery levin
May your thin, withered, wrinkled neck be broke!
   " 'You say that dripping eaves, and also smoke,
And wives contentious, will make men to flee
Out of their houses; ah, *benedicite!*
What ails such an old fellow so to chide?
   " 'You say that all we wives our vices hide
Till we are married, then we show them well;
That is a scoundrel's proverb, let me tell!
   " 'You say that oxen, asses, horses, hounds
Are tried out variously, and on good grounds;
Basins and bowls, before men will them buy,
And spoons and stools and all such goods you try.
And so with pots and clothes and all array;
But of their wives men get no trial, you say,
Till they are married, base old dotard you!
And then we show what evil we can do.
   " 'You say also that it displeases me
Unless you praise and flatter my beauty,
And save you gaze always upon my face
And call me "lovely lady" every place;
And save you make a feast upon that day
When I was born, and give me garments gay;
And save due honour to my nurse is paid
As well as to my faithful chambermaid,
And to my father's folk and his allies —
Thus you go on, old barrel full of lies!
   " 'And yet of our apprentice, young Jenkin,
For his crisp hair, showing like gold so fine,
Because he squires me walking up and down,
A false suspicion in your mind is sown;
I'd give him naught, though you were dead tomorrow.
   " 'But tell me this, why do you hide, with sorrow,
The keys to your strong-box away from me?
It is my gold as well as yours, pardie.
Why would you make an idiot of your dame?
Now by Saint James, but you shall miss your aim,
You shall not be, although like mad you scold,
Master of both my body and my gold;
One you'll forgo in spite of both your eyes;
Why need you seek me out or set on spies?

I think you'd like to lock me in your chest!
You should say: "Dear wife, go where you like best,
Amuse yourself, I will believe no tales;
You're my wife Alis true, and truth prevails."
We love no man that guards us or gives charge
Of where we go, for we will be at large.
    " 'Of all men the most blessed may he be,
That wise astrologer, Dan Ptolemy,
Who says this proverb in his Almagest:
"Of all men he's in wisdom the highest
That nothing cares who has the world in hand."
And by this proverb shall you understand:
Since you've enough, why do you reck or care
How merrily all other folks may fare?
For certainly, old dotard, by your leave,
You shall have cunt all right enough at eve.
He is too much a niggard who's so tight
That from his lantern he'll give none a light.
For he'll have never the less light, by gad;
Since you've enough, you need not be so sad.
    " 'You say, also, that if we make us gay
With clothing, all in costliest array,
That it's a danger to our chastity;
And you must back the saying up, pardie!
Repeating these words in the apostle's name:
"In habits meet for chastity, not shame,
Your women shall be garmented," said he,
"And not with broidered hair, or jewellery,
Or pearls, or gold, or costly gowns and chic;"
After your text and after your rubric
I will not follow more than would a gnat.
You said this, too, that I was like a cat;
For if one care to singe a cat's furred skin,
Then would the cat remain the house within;
And if the cat's coat be all sleek and gay,
She will not keep in house a half a day,
But out she'll go, ere dawn of any day,
To show her skin and caterwaul and play.
This is to say, if I'm a little gay,
To show my rags I'll gad about all day.
    " 'Sir Ancient Fool, what ails you with your spies?

Though you pray Argus, with his hundred eyes,
To be my body-guard and do his best,
Faith, he sha'n't hold me, save I am modest;
I could delude him easily — trust me!
    " 'You said, also, that there are three things — three —
The which things are a trouble on this earth,
And that no man may ever endure the fourth:
O dear Sir Rogue, may Christ cut short your life!
Yet do you preach and say a hateful wife
Is to be reckoned one of these mischances.
Are there no other kinds of resemblances
That you may liken thus your parables to,
But must a hapless wife be made to do?
    " 'You liken woman's love to very Hell,
To desert land where waters do not well.
You liken it, also, unto wildfire;
The more it burns, the more it has desire
To consume everything that burned may be.
You say that just as worms destroy a tree,
Just so a wife destroys her own husband;
Men know this who are bound in marriage band.'
    "Masters, like this, as you must understand,
Did I my old men charge and censure, and
Claim that they said these things in drunkenness;
And all was false, but yet I took witness
Of Jenkin and of my dear niece also.
O Lord, the pain I gave them and the woe,
All guiltless, too, by God's grief exquisite!
For like a stallion could I neigh and bite.
I could complain, though mine was all the guilt,
Or else, full many a time, I'd lost the tilt.
Whoso comes first to mill first gets meal ground;
I whimpered first and so did them confound.
They were right glad to hasten to excuse
Things they had never done, save in my ruse.
    "With wenches would I charge him, by this hand,
When, for some illness, he could hardly stand.
Yet tickled this the heart of him, for he
Deemed it was love produced such jealousy.
I swore that all my walking out at night
Was but to spy on girls he kept outright;

And under cover of that I had much mirth.
For all such wit is given us at birth;
Deceit, weeping, and spinning, does God give
To women, naturally, the while they live.
And thus of one thing I speak boastfully,
I got the best of each one, finally,
By trick, or force, or by some kind of thing,
As by continual growls or murmuring;
Especially in bed had they mischance,
There would I chide and give them no pleasance;
I would no longer in the bed abide
If I but felt his arm across my side,
Till he had paid his ransom unto me;
Then would I let him do his nicety.
And therefore to all men this tale I tell,
Let gain who may, for everything's to sell.
With empty hand men may no falcons lure;
For profit would I all his lust endure,
And make for him a well-feigned appetite;
Yet I in bacon never had delight;
And that is why I used so much to chide.
For if the pope were seated there beside
I'd not have spared them, no, at their own board.
For by my truth, I paid them, word for word.
So help me the True God Omnipotent,
Though I right now should make my testament,
I owe them not a word that was not quit.
I brought it so about, and by my wit,
That they must give it up, as for the best,
Or otherwise we'd never have had rest.
For though he glared and scowled like lion mad,
Yet failed he of the end he wished he had.
    "Then would I say: 'Good dearie, see you keep
In mind how meek is Wilkin, our old sheep;
Come near, my spouse, come let me kiss your cheek!
You should be always patient, aye, and meek,
And have a sweetly scrupulous tenderness,
Since you so preach of old Job's patience, yes.
Suffer always, since you so well can preach;
And, save you do, be sure that we will teach
That it is well to leave a wife in peace.

One of us two must bow, to be at ease;
And since a man's more reasonable, they say,
Than woman is, you must have patience aye.
What ails you that you grumble thus and groan?
Is it because you'd have my cunt alone?
Why take it all, lo, have it every bit;
Peter! Beshrew you but you're fond of it!
For if I would go peddle my *belle chose*,
I could walk out as fresh as is a rose;
But I will keep it for your own sweet tooth.
You are to blame, by God I tell the truth.'
    "Such were the words I had at my command.
Now will I tell you of my fourth husband.
    "My fourth husband, he was a reveller,
That is to say, he kept a paramour;
And young and full of passion then was I,
Stubborn and strong and jolly as a pie.
Well could I dance to tune of harp, nor fail
To sing as well as any nightingale
When I had drunk a good draught of sweet wine.
Metellius, the foul churl and the swine,
Did with a staff deprive his wife of life
Because she drank wine; had I been his wife
He never should have frightened me from drink;
For after wine, of Venus must I think:
For just as surely as cold produces hail,
A liquorish mouth must have a lickerish tail.
In women wine's no bar of impotence,
This know all lechers by experience.
    "But Lord Christ! When I do remember me
Upon my youth and on my jollity,
It tickles me about my heart's deep root.
To this day does my heart sing in salute
That I have had my world in my own time.
But age, alas! that poisons every prime,
Has taken away my beauty and my pith;
Let go, farewell, the devil go therewith!
The flour is gone, there is no more to tell,
The bran, as best I may, must I now sell;
But yet to be right merry I'll try, and
Now will I tell you of my fourth husband.

"I say that in my heart I'd great despite
When he of any other had delight;
But he was quit, by God and by Saint Joce!
I made, of the same wood, a staff most gross;
Not with my body and in manner foul,
But certainly I showed so gay a soul
That in his own thick grease I made him fry
For anger and for utter jealousy.
By God, on earth I was his purgatory,
For which I hope his soul lives now in glory.
For God knows, many a time he sat and sung
When the shoe bitterly his foot had wrung.
There was no one, save God and he, that knew
How, in so many ways, I'd twist the screw.
He died when I came from Jerusalem,
And lies entombed beneath the great rood-beam,
Although his tomb is not so glorious
As was the sepulchre of Darius,
The which Apelles wrought full cleverly;
'Twas waste to bury him expensively.
Let him fare well. God give his soul good rest,
He now is in the grave and in his chest.
    "And now of my fifth husband will I tell.
God grant his soul may never get to Hell!
And yet he was to me most brutal, too;
My ribs yet feel as they were black and blue,
And ever shall, until my dying day.
But in our bed he was so fresh and gay,
And therewithal he could so well impose,
What time he wanted use of my *belle chose*,
That though he'd beaten me on every bone,
He could re-win my love, and that full soon.
I guess I loved him best of all, for he
Gave of his love most sparingly to me.
We women have, if I am not to lie,
In this love matter, a quaint fantasy;
Look out a thing we may not lightly have,
And after that we'll cry all day and crave.
Forbid a thing, and that thing covet we;
Press hard upon us, then we turn and flee.
Sparingly offer we our goods, when fair;

Great crowds at market make for dearer ware,
And what's too common brings but little price;
All this knows every woman who is wise.
   "My fifth husband, may God his spirit bless!
Whom I took all for love, and not riches,
Had been sometime a student at Oxford,
And had left school and had come home to board
With my best gossip, dwelling in our town,
God save her soul! Her name was Alison.
She knew my heart and all my privity
Better than did our parish priest, s'help me!
To her confided I my secrets all.
For had my husband pissed against a wall,
Or done a thing that might have cost his life,
To her and to another worthy wife,
And to my niece whom I loved always well,
I would have told it — every bit I'd tell,
And did so, many and many a time, God wot,
Which made his face full often red and hot
For utter shame; he blamed himself that he
Had told me of so deep a privity.
   "So it befell that on a time, in Lent
(For oftentimes I to my gossip went,
Since I loved always to be glad and gay
And to walk out, in March, April, and May,
From house to house, to hear the latest malice),
Jenkin the clerk, and my gossip Dame Alis,
And I myself into the meadows went.
My husband was in London all that Lent;
I had the greater leisure, then, to play,
And to observe, and to be seen, I say,
By pleasant folk; what knew I where my face
Was destined to be loved, or in what place?
Therefore I made my visits round about
To vigils and processions of devout,
To preaching too, and shrines of pilgrimage,
To miracle plays, and always to each marriage,
And wore my scarlet skirt before all wights.
These worms and all these moths and all these mites,
I say it at my peril, never ate;
And know you why? I wore it early and late.

"Now will I tell you what befell to me.
I say that in the meadows walked we three
Till, truly, we had come to such dalliance,
This clerk and I, that, of my vigilance,
I spoke to him and told him how that he,
Were I a widow, might well marry me.
For certainly I say it not to brag,
But I was never quite without a bag
Full of the needs of marriage that I seek.
I hold a mouse's heart not worth a leek
That has but one hole into which to run,
And if it fail of that, then all is done.
"I made him think he had enchanted me;
My mother taught me all that subtlety.
And then I said I'd dreamed of him all night,
He would have slain me as I lay upright,
And all my bed was full of very blood;
But yet I hoped that he would do me good,
For blood betokens gold, as I was taught.
And all was false, I dreamed of him just — naught,
Save as I acted on my mother's lore,
As well in this thing as in many more.
"But now, let's see, what was I going to say?
Aha, by God, I know! It goes this way.
"When my fourth husband lay upon his bier,
I wept enough and made but sorry cheer,
As wives must always, for it's custom's grace,
And with my kerchief covered up my face;
But since I was provided with a mate,
I really wept but little, I may state.
"To church my man was borne upon the morrow
By neighbours, who for him made signs of sorrow,
And Jenkin, our good clerk, was one of them.
So help me God, when rang the requiem
After the bier, I thought he had a pair
Of legs and feet so clean-cut and so fair
That all my heart I gave to him to hold.
He was, I think, but twenty winters old,
And I was forty, if I tell the truth;
But then I always had a young colt's tooth.
Gap-toothed I was, and that became me well;

I had the print of holy Venus' seal.
So help me God, I was a healthy one,
And fair and rich and young and full of fun;
And truly, as my husbands all told me,
I had the silkiest *quoniam*[2] that could be.
For truly, I am all Venusian
In feeling, and my brain is Martian.
Venus gave me my lust, my lickerishness,
And Mars gave me my sturdy hardiness.
Taurus was my ascendant, with Mars therein.
Alas, alas, that ever love was sin!
I followed always my own inclination
By virtue of my natal constellation;
Which wrought me so I never could withdraw
My Venus-chamber from a good fellow.
Yet have I Mars's mark upon my face,
And also in another private place.
For God so truly my salvation be
As I have never loved for policy,
But ever followed my own appetite,
Though he were short or tall, or black or white;
I took no heed, so that he cared for me,
How poor he was, nor even of what degree.
    "What should I say now, save, at the month's end,
This jolly, gentle, Jenkin clerk, my friend,
Had wedded me full ceremoniously,
And to him gave I all the land in fee
That ever had been given me before;
But later I repented me full sore.
He never suffered me to have my way.
By God, he smote me on the ear, one day,
Because I tore out of his book a leaf;
So that from this my ear is grown quite deaf.
Stubborn I was as is a lioness,
And with my tongue a very jay, I guess,
And walk I would, as I had done before,
From house to house, though I should not, he swore.
For which he oftentimes would sit and preach
And read old Roman tales to me and teach

2. quoniam] pudendum.

How one Sulpicius Gallus left his wife
And her forsook for term of all his life
Because he saw her with bared head, I say,
Looking out from his door, upon a day.
    "Another Roman told he of by name
Who, since his wife was at a summer-game
Without his knowing, he forsook her eke.
And then would he within his Bible seek
That proverb of the old Ecclesiast
Where he commands so freely and so fast
That man forbid his wife to gad about;
Then would he thus repeat, with never doubt:
    'Whoso would build his whole house out of sallows,
    And spur his blind horse to run over fallows,
    And let his wife alone go seeking hallows,
    Is worthy to be hanged upon the gallows.'
But all for naught, I didn't care a haw
For all his proverbs, nor for his old saw, .
Nor yet would I by him corrected be.
I hate one that my vices tells to me,
And so do more of us — God knows! — than I.
This made him mad with me, and furiously,
That I'd not yield to him in any case.
    "Now will I tell you truth, by Saint Thomas,
Of why I tore from out his book a leaf,
For which he struck me so it made me deaf.
    "He had a book that gladly, night and day,
For his amusement he would read alway.
He called it 'Theophrastus' and 'Valerius',
At which book would he laugh, uproarious.
And, too, there sometime was a clerk at Rome,
A cardinal, that men called Saint Jerome,
Who made a book against Jovinian;
In which book, too, there was Tertullian,
Chrysippus, Trotula, and Heloïse
Who was abbess near Paris' diocese;
And too, the *Proverbs* of King Solomon,
And Ovid's *Art*, and books full many a one.
And all of these were bound in one volume.
And every night and day 'twas his custom,
When he had leisure and took some vacation

From all his other worldly occupation,
To read, within this book, of wicked wives.
He knew of them more legends and more lives
Than are of good wives written in the Bible.
For trust me, it's impossible, no libel,
That any cleric shall speak well of wives,
Unless it be of saints and holy lives,
But naught for other women will they do.
Who painted first the lion,[3] tell me who?
By God, if women had but written stories,
As have these clerks within their oratories,
They would have written of men more wickedness
Than all the race of Adam could redress.
The children of Mercury and of Venus
Are in their lives antagonistic thus;
For Mercury loves wisdom and science, .
And Venus loves but pleasure and expense.
Because they different dispositions own,
Each falls when other's in ascendant shown.
And God knows Mercury is desolate
In Pisces, wherein Venus rules in state;
And Venus falls when Mercury is raised;
Therefore no woman by a clerk is praised.
A clerk, when he is old and can naught do
Of Venus' labours worth his worn-out shoe,
Then sits he down and writes, in his dotage,
That women cannot keep vow of marriage!
    "But now to tell you, as I started to,
Why I was beaten for a book, *pardieu*.
Upon a night Jenkin, who was our sire,
Read in his book, as he sat by the fire,
Of Mother Eve who, by her wickedness,
First brought mankind to all his wretchedness,
For which Lord Jesus Christ Himself was slain,
Who, with His heart's blood, saved us thus again.
Lo here, expressly of woman, may you find

3. *Who . . . lion*] in one of Aesop's fables, a lion is shown a picture of a man killing a lion, whereupon he explains that if a lion had painted the picture, the roles would have been reversed.

That woman was the ruin of mankind.

"Then read he out how Samson lost his hairs,
Sleeping, his leman[4] cut them with her shears;
And through this treason lost he either eye.

"Then read he out, if I am not to lie,
Of Hercules, and Deianira's desire
That caused him to go set himself on fire.[5]

"Nothing escaped him of the pain and woe
That Socrates had with his spouses two;
How Xantippe threw piss upon his head;
This hapless man sat still, as he were dead;
He wiped his head, no more durst he complain
Than 'Ere the thunder ceases comes the rain.'

"Then of Pasiphaë,[6] the queen of Crete,
For cursedness he thought the story sweet;
Fie! Say no more — it is an awful thing —
Of her so horrible lust and love-liking.

"Of Clytemnestra, for her lechery,
Who caused her husband's death by treachery,
He read all this with greatest zest, I vow.

"He told me, too, just when it was and how
Amphiaraus at Thebes lost his life;
My husband had a legend of his wife
Eriphyle who, for a brooch of gold,
In secrecy to hostile Greeks had told
Whereat her husband had his hiding place,
For which he found at Thebes but sorry grace.

"Of Livia and Lucia told he me,
For both of them their husbands killed, you see,
The one for love, the other killed for hate;
Livia her husband, on an evening late,
Made drink some poison, for she was his foe.
Lucia, lecherous, loved her husband so
That, to the end he'd always of her think,
She gave him such a philtre, for love-drink,
That he was dead or ever it was morrow;
And husbands thus, by same means, came to sorrow.

4. *leman*] mistress.
5. *Hercules . . . fire*] Deianira unknowingly gave Hercules a poisoned shirt that was so
   painful he committed suicide by fire.
6. *Pasiphaë*] fell in love with a bull and gave birth to the Minotaur.

"Then did he tell how one Latumius
Complained unto his comrade Arrius
That in his garden grew a baleful tree
Whereon, he said, his wives, and they were three,
Had hanged themselves for wretchedness and woe.
'O brother,' Arrius said, 'and did they so?
Give me a graft of that same blessed tree
And in my garden planted it shall be!'
    "Of wives of later date he also read,
How some had slain their husbands in their bed
And let their lovers shag them all the night
While corpses lay upon the floor upright.
And some had driven nails into the brain
While husbands slept and in such wise were slain.
And some had given them poison in their drink.
He told more evil than the mind can think.
And therewithal he knew of more proverbs
Than in this world there grows of grass or herbs.
'Better,' he said, 'your habitation be
With lion wild or dragon foul,' said he,
'Than with a woman who will nag and chide.'
'Better,' he said, 'on the housetop abide
Than with a brawling wife down in the house;
Such are so wicked and contrarious
They hate the thing their husband loves, for aye.'
He said, 'a woman throws her shame away
When she throws off her smock,' and further, too:
'A woman fair, save she be chaste also,
Is like a ring of gold in a sow's nose.'
Who would imagine or who would suppose
What grief and pain were in this heart of mine?
    "And when I saw he'd never cease, in fine,
His reading in this cursed book at night,
Three leaves of it I snatched and tore outright
Out of his book, as he read on; and eke[7]
I with my fist so took him on the cheek,
That in our fire he reeled and fell right down.
Then he got up as does a wild lion,
And with his fist he struck me on the head,

7. *eke*] also.

And on the floor I lay as I were dead.
And when he saw how limp and still I lay,
He was afraid and would have run away,
Until at last out of my swoon I made:
'Oh, have you slain me, you false thief?' I said,
'And for my land have you thus murdered me?
Kiss me before I die, and let me be.'
    "He came to me and near me he knelt down,
And said: 'O my dear sister Alison,
So help me God, I'll never strike you more;
What I have done, you are to blame therefor.
But all the same forgiveness now I seek!'
And thereupon I hit him on the cheek,
And said: 'Thief, so much vengeance do I wreak!
Now will I die, I can no longer speak!'
But at the last, and with much care and woe,
We made it up between ourselves. And so
He put the bridle reins within my hand
To have the governing of house and land;
And of his tongue and of his hand, also;
And made him burn his book, right then, oho!
And when I had thus gathered unto me
Masterfully, the entire sovereignty,
And he had said: 'My own true wedded wife,
Do as you please the term of all your life,
Guard your own honour and keep fair my state' —
After that day we never had debate.
God help me now, I was to him as kind
As any wife from Denmark unto Ind,
And also true, and so was he to me.
I pray to God, Who sits in majesty,
To bless his soul, out of His mercy dear!
Now will I tell my tale, if you will hear."

Behold the Words Between
the Summoner and the Friar

The friar laughed when he had heard all this.
"Now dame," said he, "so have I joy or bliss
This is a long preamble to a tale!"
    And when the summoner heard this friar's hail,
"Lo," said the summoner, "by God's arms two!
A friar will always interfere, mark you.
Behold, good men, a housefly and a friar
Will fall in every dish and matters higher.
Why speak of preambling, you in your gown?
What! Amble, trot, hold peace, or go sit down;
You hinder our diversion thus to inquire."
    "Aye, say you so, sir summoner?" said the friar,
"Now by my faith I will, before I go,
Tell of a summoner such a tale, or so,
That all the folk shall laugh who're in this place."
    "Otherwise, friar, I beshrew your face,"
Replied this summoner, "and beshrew me
If I do not tell tales here, two or three,
Of friars ere I come to Sittingbourne,
That certainly will give you cause to mourn,
For well I know your patience will be gone."
    Our host cried out, "Now peace, and that anon!"
And said he: "Let the woman tell her tale.
You act like people who are drunk with ale.
Do, lady, tell your tale, and that is best."
    "All ready, sir," said she, "as you request,
If I have license of this worthy friar."
    "Yes, dame," said he, "to hear you's my desire."

Here the Wife of Bath Ends Her Prologue

THE TALE OF THE WIFE OF BATH

NOW IN THE OLDEN days of King Arthur,
Of whom the Britons speak with great honour,
All this wide land was land of faëry.
The elf-queen, with her jolly company,
Danced oftentimes on many a green mead;
This was the old opinion, as I read.
I speak of many hundred years ago;
But now no man can see the elves, you know.
For now the so-great charity and prayers
Of limiters and other holy friars
That do infest each land and every stream
As thick as motes are in a bright sunbeam,
Blessing halls, chambers, kitchens, ladies' bowers,
Cities and towns and castles and high towers,
Manors and barns and stables, aye and dairies —
This causes it that there are now no fairies.
For where was wont to walk full many an elf,
Right there walks now the limiter himself
In noons and afternoons and in mornings,
Saying his matins and such holy things,
As he goes round his district in his gown.
Women may now go safely up and down,
In every copse or under every tree;
There is no other incubus than he,
And would do them nothing but dishonour.
  And so befell it that this King Arthur
Had at his court a lusty bachelor
Who, on a day, came riding from river;[1]
And happened that, alone as she was born,
He saw a maiden walking through the corn,
From whom, in spite of all she did and said,
Straightway by force he took her maidenhead;
For which violation was there such clamour,

1. *from river*] from hawking for waterfowl beside a stream or mere.

And such appealing unto King Arthur,
That soon condemned was this knight to be dead
By course of law, and should have lost his head,
Peradventure, such being the statute then;
But that the other ladies and the queen
So long prayed of the king to show him grace,
He granted life, at last, in the law's place,
And gave him to the queen, as she should will,
Whether she'd save him, or his blood should spill.

The queen she thanked the king with all her might,
And after this, thus spoke she to the knight,
When she'd an opportunity, one day:
"You stand yet," said she, "in such poor a way
That for your life you've no security.
I'll grant you life if you can tell to me
What thing it is that women most desire.
Be wise, and keep your neck from iron dire!
And if you cannot tell it me anon,
Then will I give you license to be gone
A twelvemonth and a day, to search and learn
Sufficient answer in this grave concern.
And your knight's word I'll have, ere forth you pace,
To yield your body to me in this place."

Grieved was this knight, and sorrowfully he sighed;
But there! he could not do as pleased his pride.
And at the last he chose that he would wend,
And come again upon the twelvemonth's end,
With such an answer as God might purvey;
And so he took his leave and went his way.

He sought out every house and every place
Wherein he hoped to find that he had grace
To learn what women love the most of all;
But nowhere ever did it him befall
To find, upon the question stated here,
Two persons who agreed with statement clear.

Some said that women all loved best riches,
Some said, fair fame, and some said, prettiness;
Some, rich array, some said 'twas lust abed
And often to be widowed and re-wed.

Some said that our poor hearts are aye most eased
When we have been most flattered and thus pleased.
And he went near the truth, I will not lie;

A man may win us best with flattery;
And with attentions and with busyness
We're often limed,[2] the greater and the less.
    And some say, too, that we do love the best
To be quite free to do our own behest,
And that no man reprove us for our vice,
But saying we are wise, take our advice.
For truly there is no one of us all,
If anyone shall rub us on a gall,
That will not kick because he tells the truth.
Try, and he'll find, who does so, I say sooth.
No matter how much vice we have within,
We would be held for wise and clean of sin.
    And some folk say that great delight have we
To be held constant, also trustworthy,
And on one purpose steadfastly to dwell,
And not betray a thing that men may tell.
But that tale is not worth a rake's handle;
By God, we women can no thing conceal,
As witness Midas. Would you hear the tale?
    Ovid, among some other matters small,
Said Midas had beneath his long curled hair,
Two ass's ears that grew in secret there,
The which defect he hid, as best he might,
Full cunningly from every person's sight,
And, save his wife, no one knew of it, no.
He loved her most, and trusted her also;
And he prayed of her that to no creature
She'd tell of his disfigurement impure.
    She swore him: Nay, for all this world to win
She would do no such villainy or sin
And cause her husband have so foul a name;
Nor would she tell it for her own deep shame.
Nevertheless, she thought she would have died
Because so long the secret must she hide;
It seemed to swell so big about her heart
That some word from her mouth must surely start;
And since she dared to tell it to no man,
Down to a marsh, that lay hard by, she ran;
Till she came there her heart was all afire,

2. *limed*] ensnared.

And as a bittern[3] booms in the quagmire,
She laid her mouth low to the water down:
"Betray me not, you sounding water blown,"
Said she, "I tell it to none else but you:
Long ears like asses' has my husband two!
Now is my heart at ease, since that is out;
I could no longer keep it, there's no doubt."
Here may you see, though for a while we bide,
Yet out it must; no secret can we hide.
The rest of all this tale, if you would hear,
Read Ovid: in his book does it appear.[4]

   This knight my tale is chiefly told about
When what he went for he could not find out,
That is, the thing that women love the best,
Most saddened was the spirit in his breast;
But home he goes, he could no more delay.
The day was come when home he turned his way;
And on his way it chanced that he should ride
In all his care, beneath a forest's side,
And there he saw, a-dancing him before,
Full four and twenty ladies, maybe more;
Toward which dance eagerly did he turn
In hope that there some wisdom he should learn.
But truly, ere he came upon them there,
The dancers vanished all, he knew not where.
No creature saw he that gave sign of life,
Save, on the greensward sitting, an old wife;
A fouler person could no man devise.
Before the knight this old wife did arise,
And said: "Sir knight, hence lies no travelled way.
Tell me what thing you seek, and by your fay.
Perchance you'll find it may the better be;
These ancient folk know many things," said she.

   "Dear mother," said this knight assuredly,
"I am but dead, save I can tell, truly,
What thing it is that women most desire;
Could you inform me, I'd pay well your hire."
   "Plight me your troth here, hand in hand," said she,

---

3. *bittern*] bird related to the heron.
4. *The rest . . . appear*] the reeds reveal the secret by whispering "*aures aselli*" (ass's ears).

"That you will do, whatever it may be,
The thing I ask if it lie in your might;
And I'll give you your answer ere the night."
    "Have here my word," said he. "That thing I grant."
    "Then," said the crone, "of this I make my vaunt,
Your life is safe; and I will stand thereby,
Upon my life, the queen will say as I.
Let's see which is the proudest of them all
That wears upon her hair kerchief or caul,[5]
Shall dare say no to that which I shall teach;
Let us go now and without longer speech."
    Then whispered she a sentence in his ear,
And bade him to be glad and have no fear.
    When they were come unto the court, this knight
Said he had kept his promise as was right,
And ready was his answer, as he said.
Full many a noble wife, and many a maid,
And many a widow, since they are so wise,
The queen herself sitting as high justice,
Assembled were, his answer there to hear;
And then the knight was bidden to appear.
    Command was given for silence in the hall,
And that the knight should tell before them all
What thing all worldly women love the best.
This knight did not stand dumb, as does a beast,
But to this question presently answered
With manly voice, so that the whole court heard:
"My liege lady, generally," said he,
"Women desire to have the sovereignty
As well upon their husband as their love,
And to have mastery their man above;
This thing you most desire, though me you kill
Do as you please, I am here at your will."
    In all the court there was no wife or maid
Or widow that denied the thing he said,
But all held, he was worthy to have life.
    And with that word up started the old wife
Whom he had seen a-sitting on the green.

5. *caul*] headdress.

"Mercy," cried she, "my sovereign lady queen!
Before the court's dismissed, give me my right.
'Twas I who taught the answer to this knight;
For which he did plight troth to me, out there,
That the first thing I should of him require
He would do that, if it lay in his might.
Before the court, now, pray I you, sir knight,"
Said she, "that you will take me for your wife;
For well you know that I have saved your life.
If this be false, say nay, upon your fay!"

This knight replied: "Alas and welaway!
That I so promised I will not protest.
But for God's love pray make a new request,
Take all my wealth and let my body go."

"Nay then," said she, "beshrew us if I do!
For though I may be foul and old and poor,
I will not, for all metal and all ore
That from the earth is dug or lies above,
Be aught except your wife and your true love."

"My love?" cried he, "nay, rather my damnation!
Alas! that any of my race and station
Should ever so dishonoured foully be!"

But all for naught; the end was this, that he
Was so constrained he needs must go and wed,
And take his ancient wife and go to bed.

Now, peradventure, would some men say here,
That, of my negligence, I take no care
To tell you of the joy and all the array
That at the wedding feast were seen that day.
Make a brief answer to this thing I shall;
I say, there was no joy or feast at all;
There was but heaviness and grievous sorrow;
For privately he wedded on the morrow,
And all day, then, he hid him like an owl;
So sad he was, his old wife looked so foul.

Great was the woe the knight had in his thought
When he, with her, to marriage bed was brought;
He rolled about and turned him to and fro.
His old wife lay there, always smiling so,
And said: "O my dear husband, *ben'cite!*
Fares every knight with wife as you with me?

Is this the custom in King Arthur's house?
Are knights of his all so fastidious?
I am your own true love and, more, your wife;
And I am she who saved your very life;
And truly, since I've never done you wrong,
Why do you treat me so, this first night long?
You act as does a man who's lost his wit;
What is my fault? For God's love tell me it,
And it shall be amended, if I may."
    "Amended!" cried this knight, "Alas, nay, nay!
It will not be amended ever, no!
You are so loathsome, and so old also,
And therewith of so low a race were born,
It's little wonder that I toss and turn.
Would God my heart would break within my breast!"
    "Is this," asked she, "the cause of your unrest?"
    "Yes, truly," said he, "and no wonder 'tis."
    "Now, sir," said she, "I could amend all this,
If I but would, and that within days three,
If you would bear yourself well towards me.
    "But since you speak of such gentility
As is descended from old wealth, till ye
Claim that for that you should be gentlemen,
I hold such arrogance not worth a hen.
Find him who is most virtuous alway,
Alone or publicly, and most tries aye
To do whatever noble deeds he can,
And take him for the greatest gentleman.
Christ wills we claim from Him gentility,
Not from ancestors of landocracy.
For though they give us all their heritage,
For which we claim to be of high lineage,
Yet can they not bequeath, in anything,
To any of us, their virtuous living,
That made men say they had gentility,
And bade us follow them in like degree.
    "Well does that poet wise of great Florence,
Called Dante, speak his mind in this sentence;
Somewhat like this may it translated be:
'Rarely unto the branches of the tree
Doth human worth mount up: and so ordains

He Who bestows it; to Him it pertains.'[6]
For of our fathers may we nothing claim
But temporal things, that man may hurt and maim.
    "And everyone knows this as well as I,
If nobleness were implanted naturally
Within a certain lineage, down the line,
In private and in public, I opine,
The ways of gentleness they'd always show
And never fall to vice and conduct low.
    "Take fire and carry it in the darkest house
Between here and the Mount of Caucasus,
And let men shut the doors and from them turn;
Yet will the fire as fairly blaze and burn
As twenty thousand men did it behold;
Its nature and its office it will hold,
On peril of my life, until it die.
    "From this you see that true gentility
Is not allied to wealth a man may own,
Since folk do not their deeds, as may be shown,
As does the fire, according to its kind.
For God knows that men may full often find ·
A lord's son doing shame and villainy;
And he that prizes his gentility
In being born of some old noble house,
With ancestors both noble and virtuous,
But will himself do naught of noble deeds
Nor follow him to whose name he succeeds,
He is not gentle, be he duke or earl; ,
For acting churlish makes a man a churl.
Gentility is not just the renown
Of ancestors who have some greatness shown,
In which you have no portion of your own.
Your own gentility comes from God alone;
Thence comes our true nobility by grace,
It was not willed us with our rank and place.
    "Think how noble, as says Valerius,
Was that same Tullius Hostilius,
Who out of poverty rose to high estate.

---

6. '*Rarely . . . pertains.*'] from *The Divine Comedy*, Purgatory VII, 122–23; this line, translated by Cary, was altered slightly here.

Seneca and Boethius inculcate,
Expressly (and no doubt it thus proceeds),
That he is noble who does noble deeds;
And therefore, husband dear, I thus conclude:
Although my ancestors mayhap were rude,
Yet may the High Lord God, and so hope I,
Grant me the grace to live right virtuously.
Then I'll be gentle when I do begin
To live in virtue and to do no sin.

   "And when you me reproach for poverty,
The High God, in Whom we believe, say I,
In voluntary poverty lived His life.
And surely every man, or maid, or wife
May understand that Jesus, Heaven's King,
Would not have chosen vileness of living.
Glad poverty's an honest thing, that's plain,
Which Seneca and other clerks maintain.
Whoso will be content with poverty,
I hold him rich, though not a shirt has he.
And he that covets much is a poor wight,
For he would gain what's all beyond his might.
But he that has not, nor desires to have,
Is rich, although you hold him but a knave.

   "True poverty, it sings right naturally;
Juvenal gaily says of poverty:
'The poor man, when he walks along the way,
Before the robbers he may sing and play.'
Poverty's odious good, and, as I guess,
It is a stimulant to busyness;
A great improver, too, of sapience
In him that takes it all with due patience.
Poverty's this, though it seem misery —
Its quality may none dispute, say I.
Poverty often, when a man is low,
Makes him his God and even himself to know.
And poverty's an eye-glass, seems to me,
Through which a man his loyal friends may see.
Since you've received no injury from me,
Then why reproach me for my poverty.

   "Now, sir, with age you have upbraided me;
And truly, sir, though no authority

Were in a book, you gentles of honour
Say that men should the aged show favour,
And call him father, of your gentleness;
And authors could I find for this, I guess.
  "Now since you say that I am foul and old,
Then fear you not to be made a cuckold;
For dirt and age, as prosperous I may be,
Are mighty wardens over chastity.
Nevertheless, since I know your delight,
I'll satisfy your worldly appetite.
  "Choose, now," said she, "one of these two things, aye,
To have me foul and old until I die,
And be to you a true and humble wife,
And never anger you in all my life;
Or else to have me young and very fair
And take your chance with those who will repair
Unto your house, and all because of me,
Or in some other place, as well may be.
Now choose which you like better and reply."
  This knight considered, and did sorely sigh,
But at the last replied as you shall hear:
"My lady and my love, and wife so dear,
I put myself in your wise governing;
Do you choose which may be the more pleasing,
And bring most honour to you, and me also;
I care not which it be of these things two;
For if you like it, that suffices me."
  "Then have I got of you the mastery,
Since I may choose and govern, in earnest?"
  "Yes, truly, wife," said he, "I hold that best."
  "Kiss me," said she, "we'll be no longer wroth,
For by my truth, to you I will be both;
That is to say, I'll be both good and fair.
I pray God I go mad, and so declare,
If I be not to you as good and true
As ever wife was since the world was new.
And, save I be, at dawn, as fairly seen
As any lady, empress, or great queen
That is between the east and the far west,
Do with my life and death as you like best.
Throw back the curtain and see how it is."

And when the knight saw verily all this,
That she so very fair was, and young too,
For joy he clasped her in his strong arms two,
His heart bathed in a bath of utter bliss;
A thousand times, all in a row, he'd kiss.
And she obeyed his wish in everything
That might give pleasure to his love-liking.
   And thus they lived unto their lives' fair end,
In perfect joy; and Jesus to us send
Meek husbands, and young ones, and fresh in bed,
And good luck to outlive them that we wed.
And I pray Jesus to cut short the lives
Of those who'll not be governed by their wives;
And old and querulous niggards with their pence,
And send them soon a mortal pestilence!

HERE ENDS THE WIFE OF BATH'S TALE

DOVER · THRIFT · EDITIONS

POETRY

THE CONGO AND OTHER POEMS, Vachel Lindsay. 96pp. 0-486-27272-9

EVANGELINE AND OTHER POEMS, Henry Wadsworth Longfellow. 64pp. 0-486-28255-4

FAVORITE POEMS, Henry Wadsworth Longfellow. 96pp. 0-486-27273-7

COMPLETE POEMS, Christopher Marlowe. 112pp. 0-486-42674-2

"TO HIS COY MISTRESS" AND OTHER POEMS, Andrew Marvell. 64pp. 0-486-29544-3

SPOON RIVER ANTHOLOGY, Edgar Lee Masters. 144pp. 0-486-27275-3

SELECTED POEMS, Claude McKay. 80pp. 0-486-40876-0

SONGS OF MILAREPA, Milarepa. 128pp. 0-486-42814-1

RENASCENCE AND OTHER POEMS, Edna St. Vincent Millay. 64pp. (Not available in Europe or the United Kingdom) 0-486-26873-X

SELECTED POEMS, John Milton. 128pp. 0-486-27554-X

CIVIL WAR POETRY: An Anthology, Paul Negri (ed.). 128pp. 0-486-29883-3

ENGLISH VICTORIAN POETRY: AN ANTHOLOGY, Paul Negri (ed.). 256pp. 0-486-40425-0

GREAT SONNETS, Paul Negri (ed.). 96pp. 0-486-28052-7

THE RAVEN AND OTHER FAVORITE POEMS, Edgar Allan Poe. 64pp. 0-486-26685-0

ESSAY ON MAN AND OTHER POEMS, Alexander Pope. 128pp. 0-486-28053-5

GOBLIN MARKET AND OTHER POEMS, Christina Rossetti. 64pp. 0-486-28055-1

CHICAGO POEMS, Carl Sandburg. 80pp. 0-486-28057-8

CORNHUSKERS, Carl Sandburg. 157pp. 0-486-41409-4

COMPLETE SONNETS, William Shakespeare. 80pp. 0-486-26686-9

SELECTED POEMS, Percy Bysshe Shelley. 128pp. 0-486-27558-2

AFRICAN-AMERICAN POETRY: An Anthology, 1773–1930, Joan R. Sherman (ed.). 96pp. 0-486-29604-0

NATIVE AMERICAN SONGS AND POEMS: An Anthology, Brian Swann (ed.). 64pp. 0-486-29450-1

SELECTED POEMS, Alfred Lord Tennyson. 112pp. 0-486-27282-6

AENEID, Vergil (Publius Vergilius Maro). 256pp. 0-486-28749-1

GREAT LOVE POEMS, Shane Weller (ed.). 128pp. 0-486-27284-2

CIVIL WAR POETRY AND PROSE, Walt Whitman. 96pp. 0-486-28507-3

SELECTED POEMS, Walt Whitman. 128pp. 0-486-26878-0

THE BALLAD OF READING GAOL AND OTHER POEMS, Oscar Wilde. 64pp. 0-486-27072-6

EARLY POEMS, William Carlos Williams. 64pp. (Available in U.S. only.) 0-486-29294-0

FAVORITE POEMS, William Wordsworth. 80pp. 0-486-27073-4

EARLY POEMS, William Butler Yeats. 128pp. 0-486-27808-5

All books complete and unabridged. All 5³⁄₁₆" x 8¼", paperbound. Available at your book dealer, online at **www.doverpublications.com**, or by writing to Dept. GI, Dover Publications, Inc., 31 East 2nd Street, Mineola, NY 11501. For current price information or for free catalogs (please indicate field of interest), write to Dover Publications or log on to **www.doverpublications.com** and see every Dover book in print. Dover publishes more than 500 books each year on science, elementary and advanced mathematics, biology, music, art, literary history, social sciences, and other areas.